PRAISE FOR
AND AN(

'Angel Creek takes me back to the heart of being twelve.
It is magical in the best possible grubby, sweaty, angel
bad-breath way. Jelly and all the other characters are so
beautifully flawed and perfect; and the sense of place and
season is sublime. What an amazing read.' Fiona Wood

'I started reading it but I couldn't stop so I read it
in a night. Things I liked a lot: the characters' names
are cool, how the angel's like a wishing thing, how it's
dark and creepy and how the angel loves Jelly. I want
to read it again.' Taya, aged 9

'I absolutely loved the book. Once I began reading it
I got stuck to it. I would rate it ten out of ten!
This book is a thrilling adventure.' Thy, Grade 6

'I think it is perfect!' Alex, Grade 6

'I really liked the story. I think the angel is cool.'
Naomi, Grade 5

'My favourite character was Pik. I liked him the best
because he was funny, he always gets into trouble.
He reminds me of my youngest brother.' Greta, Grade 6

'I like *Angel Creek* because of the excitement
and spookiness.' Asuini, Grade 3

Sally Rippin was born in Darwin, but grew up mainly in South-East Asia. Her novel *Chenxi and the Foreigner* was inspired by her time as a student in China. Now Sally lives in Melbourne, near the Merri Creek, where she writes and illustrates for children of all ages. Sally has over forty books published, many of them award-winning. She and her family spend a lot of time down by the creek, but have yet to spot an angel. She feels sure it is only a matter of time.

sallyrippin.com

ANGEL CREEK

SALLY RIPPIN

TEXT PUBLISHING *t* MELBOURNE AUSTRALIA

textpublishing.com.au
sallyrippin.com

The Text Publishing Company
Swann House
22 William Street
Melbourne Victoria 3000
Australia

First published by The Text Publishing Company, 2011
Reprinted 2012

Cover by WH Chong
Page design by Susan Miller
Typeset in Bembo 12.5/17.5 pt by J & M Typesetting
Printed and bound in Australia by Griffin Press

National Library of Australia Cataloguing-in-Publication entry:

Author: Rippin, Sally.

Title: Angel creek / Sally Rippin.

Edition: 1st ed.

ISBN: 9781921758058 (pbk.)

ISBN: 9781921834288 (ebook)

Target Audience: For primary school age.

Dewey Number: A823.3

The paper this book is printed on is certified against the Forest Stewardship Council® Standards. Griffin Press holds FSC chain of custody certification SGS-COC-005088. FSC promotes environmentally responsible, socially beneficial and economically viable management of the world's forests.

In memory of

Mikaël Rohan

the third musketeer

10.7.1996 – 16.11.2010

1

the apricot tree

There were only two things Jelly liked about the house on Rosemary Street: the creek that ran behind her back fence and the apricot tree.

Perched in the tree's wide branches, high above the garden, Jelly could see the whole world and nobody could see her. Since they had moved house, this had become Jelly's secret place. Here nobody bothered her except for the birds.

She gazed up through the shivering leaves. Pale stars glittered in the darkening sky and a huge yellow moon hung on the horizon. It was Christmas Eve. It should have been a perfect night. But Jelly was in the wrong garden in the wrong neighbourhood—perhaps even in the wrong family. Below, her parents were laughing with their new neighbours like they were having the best time in the world. Like they didn't care one bit that they'd dragged Jelly ten suburbs away from all of her friends. Even though she spoke to them almost every day, the calls only made Jelly feel worse. Tonight everyone was meeting up. Everyone except Jelly, stuck in this tree on the other side of the city. She might as well have been on the other side of the world.

She picked at a piece of bark and glared at their new house, a falling-down old weatherboard with blistered paint and sprouting gutters. Behind her, Nonna's granny flat squatted gloomily among the ragged rose bushes. Even the fairy lights her mum had strung all around the garden couldn't brighten Jelly's mood. She stretched and sighed. If she peered out over the back fence she could see the place where everything dropped away into blackness. There, in the dark, flowed the Merri Creek. From her place in the tree, she liked to imagine she could smell the cold, muddy dampness, hear the gulping of the water over the stones and the crick of the summer frogs— imagine she was someplace else.

'Hey!'

Jelly's dreaming was interrupted by a voice calling from below. She peered through the apricot leaves and saw her cousins, Gino and Pik, staring up at her. Pik was chewing on his fingers as usual, his sooty black hair sticking up everywhere. Gino's legs stuck out of his shorts like chopsticks. Every summer he shot up like a bean sprout, and now he was taller than Jelly, though he was a year younger.

'Hey,' he called again. 'Aren't you supposed to be looking after us?'

Jelly frowned. She swung down through the branches, landing in front of the boys with a soft thud.

'You're nearly as old as me, Gino. You can look after yourself.'

Gino glared at her. 'Mum and Dad said you're in charge. And besides, I don't want to get stuck with Pik and Sophia on my own.'

Jelly didn't want to get stuck looking after Gino's baby sister either. 'I hate these stupid Christmas parties,' she said, lobbing an apricot into the vegetable patch.

'Me too.' Gino kicked at the dirt.

'Me too!' said Pik.

Jelly glanced over at the back fence and drew closer to the boys. 'We could go down to the creek,' she whispered. 'That is, if you dare?'

'Cool,' said Gino, grinning.

'Cool,' said Pik, but his voice came out as a squeak.

'You sure, Pikky? It'll be dark down there,' said Jelly.

'I'm not scared.'

'There might be monsters,' Gino teased.

Pik glanced up at Jelly.

'Nah, only birds and frogs down at the creek, Pikster. Come on, we'll climb over the fence behind Nonna's flat. She's in the kitchen. No one will see us there.'

Jelly slipped away from the fairy lights into the gathering shadows at the end of the garden.

They crept through Nonna's vegetable patch, ducking between the tomato plants lined up like rows of watchful soldiers. When they reached the fence Jelly pulled Gino and Pik into the small dark space behind the granny flat.

'A kid drowned in this creek two years back,' she warned them. 'Our neighbour Maureen told us. He was playing in the drains and the water just came rushing down.' She paused for added drama. 'They never found him again.'

'Cool,' Gino said in a low voice.

'Cool,' said Pik, sticking his fingers back into his mouth.

Jelly grinned. 'Sure you don't want to go back to the house, Pikky?'

Pik shook his head.

'Come on then,' she said, and swung herself up and over the fence in one swift movement. The boys followed.

On the other side of the fence it was dark and there was no one around. The party seemed miles away, drowned out by the rushing water and the whispering of the shaggy peppercorn trees. They stood still for a moment, their backs against the fence, waiting for their eyes to adjust to the moonlight. In front of them the bank plunged towards a muddy walking track, which ran all the way along the creek. Jelly shimmied down the crumbling embankment, then beckoned to the boys.

There had been rain in the last few days and the creek was flowing fast. All the rubbish from the suburbs was pushed up onto the banks or caught up in the reeds. They followed the creek, prodding at the tangles of plastic and string, searching for any unexpected treasures.

A little way downstream, where the main road crossed the creek, the track split in two. They stopped. One path sloped up towards the bright lights of St Peter's Road; the other ran alongside the creek as it flowed through a tunnel, and was swallowed by the dark. At night the tunnel yawned blackly, like the mouth of a beast.

Jelly turned to her cousins, a smile creeping across her face. 'Shall we go in?'

'Nah,' said Pik. 'Let's go back home.'

Gino's eyes narrowed. 'You scared?'

'Of course not!'

'Then let's go.' Gino pushed past Jelly to lead the way.

The smell of pigeon poo and rotting weeds was stifling in the muggy air. Pik put his hand over his mouth. 'Stinks,' he said, gagging. He hovered in the entrance of the tunnel, where the lamps from the street above cast reassuring pools of light. Jelly followed Gino into the dark.

'Can you see?' Gino whispered.

'Sort of.' She could just make out scribbles of graffiti along the sloping walls. *Budge woz ere* and *JZ rulz* and a painting of a small yellow bird with a red beak. She ran her fingers along the ragged bluestone as

Gino ventured into the darkness.

'Hey, Jel, look at this.'

She walked to where Gino was peering out over the black water. 'I can't see anything. What is it?'

'Over there.' Gino pointed. And then Jelly saw it: a pearly smudge of white against the gloom.

'Looks like feathers,' Gino said.

'Maybe it's a bird,' said Jelly, 'caught up in all the rubbish. Poor thing.'

'I want to go back now,' Pik called. Jelly and Gino ignored him and crept closer to the edge of the creek, over the sticky mud and slimy rocks, to see if the bird-thing was alive.

'Is it moving?' Jelly whispered.

Gino shrugged.

From where they stood, it looked like it was trapped behind a large rock jutting out of the water.

'Let's go and see.' Gino stepped into the creek.

'Gino…'

'It might still be alive.'

Jelly hesitated, then rolled up her shorts. If her dad was here he would've done the same thing. He was always rescuing birds, and bugs and other creepy-crawlies. And Gino was already halfway to the rock, the water rushing past his knees. She didn't have a choice.

'What are you doing?' Pik called. 'I'll tell.'

Jelly glared at him. 'Just stay there, Pik. We'll be back in a minute.' Then she stepped into the cold water, and the mud oozed between her toes. 'Wait for me, would you?' She waded after Gino.

The water wasn't deep but the current was strong, and it pulled at her legs. She grabbed at the reeds to steady herself. When she looked up again, Gino had reached the rock. She watched him climb onto it and peer over the edge. Suddenly he reeled back, his arms like windmills.

'Jelly,' he gasped. 'It's not a bird!'

something in the water

Gino slid off the rock and lurched back through the water. On the bank Pik started to bawl.

'What is it?' Jelly called. 'What did you see?'

'Go look yourself.' Gino voice was snagged with fear.

Jelly's heart thumped. All her instincts told her to turn back—back to where the Christmas lights beckoned and her mum and dad were laughing, unaware that she had slipped out into the night. But, despite her fear, something pulled her forward, on towards the thing in the water. She had to see it for herself.

She climbed up onto the rock to gaze into the dark water on the other side.

There in the shadowy depths was a pale, pale child with glass-like eyes that stared up at her, and long white hair that billowed like clouds. It rocked gently under the water, a thin white dress caught up around its knees. And it had wings. Great white feathered wings like a pelican's, one of them bunched up and tangled in river rubbish.

Jelly felt her heart slide sideways. 'Wait.' She realised what she was seeing. 'Gino, Pik, come back.'

She heard them stop.

'What is it?' Gino called.

Jelly looked back at the creature. It was still there. Her eyes hadn't been playing tricks on her. 'You won't believe this,' she said, laughter bursting up through her chest. 'I think...I think we've found an angel!'

The angel watched her with frightened eyes. Little bubbles floated from the corners of its heart-shaped mouth and popped on the surface of the water. Its hands curled open and closed like seaweed. Jelly perched on the rock and bent forward to free its wing. But when she pulled at the knotted shreds of plastic, the other wing came thrashing out of the water.

'Hey,' she said. 'Keep still. I'm trying to help you.' She stroked the tangled wing feathers and the angel stared back at her, goggle-eyed, its peaked chest palpitating like that of a frightened bird.

The boys were hovering at the mouth of the tunnel.

'Come and see,' Jelly called, but Pik pulled away from Gino and crouched against the ragged wall.

'Stay there,' Gino said, and splashed through the water.

'Shh,' Jelly said as he approached. 'You'll scare it.' She watched him as he peered over the rock, his eyes widening.

'A real angel.' He smiled.

'I know. Can you believe it?'

Gino nudged the angel gently with his toe. Its body stiffened and its fingers curled. 'What's an angel doing here? In a creek?'

Jelly shrugged. 'Its wing's all caught up. I think it's stuck down there.'

'I want to go home,' Pik wailed into the darkness.

Gino turned. 'I told you if I let you come with us you weren't allowed to act like a baby, Pik.'

'We can't leave it there,' Jelly said. 'It might die. Or something might get it. A fox or something.'

'What would a fox do with an angel?'

'I don't know, Gino. Hold it still and I'll untie the wing.'

Gino recoiled. 'How about you hold it still and I untie the wing?'

'It doesn't have germs.'

'How do you know?'

Jelly sighed and pushed up her sleeves. The angel watched her with its spooky eyes. She inched her hands forward, then grabbed at an ankle. The angel slipped easily from her grasp.

'It's all right,' she cooed and stepped closer. The angel was the size of a small child but skinny as a pile of sticks. This time she caught it around the chest. The angel writhed, trying to get free, its spindly legs kicking up out of the water like rudders.

'Hurry, Gino. I don't know how long I can hold it.'

Gino made a grab for the tangled wing. As he touched the feathers the angel's head burst out of the water. A terrible sound like the squeal of metal filled the tunnel.

'You're hurting it!' The sound was unbearable. It took everything Jelly had not to drop the angel and cover her ears.

'Hold it still.' Gino pulled frantically at the strings of coloured plastic.

'I'm trying,' Jelly said. But the angel was as slippery as a fish.

Finally Gino pulled the last piece of plastic from the damaged wing. The angel was free. It stopped screaming and hurtled forward, clasping its arms and legs around Jelly's waist and pressing its wet face into her neck. Jelly let go of the angel, but it clung to her, its bony fingers digging into her back.

'It's got me! Get it off! Get it off!'

Gino splashed around, darting his hands in and out.

'What are you doing?' Jelly yelled. She tried to pull the angel off herself, but it only clung on tighter.

Jelly's mind was fizzing. She sucked in a mouthful of the clammy air and concentrated on slowing her breathing. She began to calm. That was when she noticed. The angel was trembling. Its whole body was quivering. 'Hey,' she said, stroking its matted hair. 'We won't hurt you.'

The angel buried its face in her neck, grunting and snuffling like a rabbit.

She looked at Gino. 'It's frightened, that's all. Poor thing.'

Gino's eyes rolled white in the dark. 'It looked like it was trying to eat you or something.'

They stood in the rushing water listening to the angel's whimpers and Pik snivelling in the dark. When the angel was quiet Gino put a hand out to touch its wing. The angel flinched, and buried its face deeper into Jelly's neck.

'Is it heavy?' Gino asked.

'No, it's really light. Must have hollow bones. Like a bird.' She patted its hair again. 'Come on then, little one. Let's get you out of the water.'

The angel's thin dress had soaked Jelly's clothes and its squeals still rang in her ears. She hitched it up and they waded to the bank. Pik had fallen quiet. His eyes were enormous, his fingers back in his mouth.

'Don't be scared, Pikky,' Jelly said. 'Look what we've found. It's an angel. A real angel!'

'Can you fix its wing?' Gino asked. 'You fixed that bird's wing that time, remember? That cockatoo.'

'Yeah,' said Jelly. 'I guess so. But what if something comes back for it? Its mother or something?'

'It can't fly,' Gino pointed out. 'It might die if we leave it here. Besides, you don't want anyone else finding it, do you?'

'No!' said Jelly. The word burst from her: she hadn't even known she was going to say it. 'All right. We'll look after it till it gets better, then we can let it go again.'

Gino grinned. 'Where are we going to keep it?'

'We can't take it back to my place. Nonna would freak. And you sure can't take it back to yours. Remember what Sophia did to your terrapins?'

Gino pulled a face. 'Don't remind me.'

'We'll have to find somewhere safe to hide it near here,' she said.

'Where?'

'I don't know. If we were at my old house I'd know plenty of places.'

'If we were at your old house we would never have found the angel. It's not like there were any creeks around there.'

'True.' Jelly hitched the angel up and walked out into the open air. She had to admit that occasionally Gino could be quite sensible.

After the dark of the tunnel the moonlit night seemed as bright as daylight. Jelly looked down at the angel, which had settled into her arms like a baby. A smile split across her face. If only her friends could see her now. She couldn't think of anyone who had found anything as special as this. She couldn't wait to see Stef's face.

As they left the tunnel behind, Pik skipped up beside her. 'Is it really an angel?' He touched its wings with sticky fingers. The angel lifted its head to look at Pik and its pointy chin bobbed on Jelly's shoulder.

'Yep. A real angel. Look, it's got wings and everything. But it's just a little one, Pikky. Just a baby who's lost its way.'

'Poor angel,' said Pik. 'What are you going to do with it, Jelly? Where are you going to put it?'

'She doesn't know yet,' Gino said. 'She's thinking.'

Jelly headed down the creek path. She always got her best ideas while walking and, to her delight, it came to her at once.

She knew the perfect place.

a place to hide

On the other side of the creek, over the road bridge, was a primary school abandoned for the summer. A tall wire fence ran all the way around the shadowy playground and the school gates were padlocked.

'There must be somewhere we can get under,' Jelly said, adjusting her hold on the angel's damp body.

The angel hunched still and silent against Jelly's chest as they walked around the fence. Its left wing was folded neatly against its spine, but the right wing hung loosely over Jelly's arm. The longest feathers almost grazed her knee. Every now and then it would lift its head to see where they were going then settle again with a sigh.

Pik trailed behind Gino, yawning and rubbing his eyes. 'Are you okay—' Jelly started to say, when a beam of light swung across a telegraph pole in front of them. A car turned into the street.

'Quick,' Jelly said to Gino. 'Grab Pik.'

She flattened herself against the fence under an enormous mulberry tree that leaned out over the footpath. Gino pulled Pik in alongside him and they huddled together, blocking the angel from view. The beam slid over the footpath in front of their feet, lighting up fat mulberries splattered across the concrete, then it passed. It wasn't until the car's tail-lights were tiny in the distance that Jelly let go of her breath and unstuck her sweaty palms from the angel's scrunched-up dress.

Pik buried his face into Jelly's hip. 'Can we go home now?'

'Soon, Pikky. Be patient.'

'Here,' Gino said. 'I've found a way in.'

The roots of the mulberry tree pushed through the wire fence and it curled away from the footpath. Gino pulled the wire upwards. The gap was wide enough for them to slide through.

'Will you get under with the angel, Jel?'

Jelly bent forward, the angel hanging off her chest. 'I don't think so. I'll go first then you can pass me the angel, Gino. Pik, you can hold up the fence.'

Jelly unhooked a spindly hand from her arm. The angel's nails had left tiny pink crescents on her skin. She tried to prise the angel away but its head jerked and its heart began to knock around in its chest. It squealed. Pik stumbled backwards, sticking his fingers into his ears. Even Gino moved away.

'Great,' Jelly shouted over the squeals. 'Thanks for your help, guys.'

In one rapid movement Jelly caught both of the angel's arms, pulled it from her and shoved it through the gap. The angel scuttled forward on all fours. Its wings flicked out and for a moment it looked like it might take off. But then its damaged wing buckled and it hurtled forward onto the concrete.

Jelly scraped her knees and elbow as she rushed under the fence, but the angel hadn't got far. When she reached it, it was huddled, shivering, against the bike racks. Jelly pulled it into her arms as Gino and Pik squeezed through the fence behind her.

'You guys are hopeless,' Jelly said.

They grinned sheepishly at her.

The three of them crept across the school grounds, reverently quiet, as if crossing the threshold of a church. A light in the hallway of a red-brick building shone a pale yellow square over a hopscotch game, marked in faded chalk on the concrete. The swings in the playground creaked.

There was something eerie about a school at night. It was like a ghost-town, ringing with the squeals of a hundred vanished children. And then Jelly heard a real shout, and the swish of bike wheels from the other side of the fence. Three boys were pedalling down the middle of the empty street, looping in and out of each other.

'Budge. Hey, Budge.'

One of them let out a wolfish howl.

'Get back,' she whispered, tugging on Pik's arm. They huddled in a doorway of the old school building.

'Did they see us?' Gino asked.

'Don't think so.' Jelly stood for a moment listening to the night: a whistle, a bird, the clacking of a tram. 'I've seen those boys around before. They're from Northbridge High, I think.'

'Your new school?'

'Unfortunately.'

Finally they spied what they were looking for—

a tool shed. Unlocked. The perfect place to keep an angel. Gino pushed open the squeaky metal door. Inside were some old paint tins, a flattened soccer ball and one lonely bike with a missing wheel. A plastic skylight let in yellow light from the streetlamps.

'The angel should be okay here,' Gino said. 'What do you think?'

'Perfect.' Jelly sat down in the corner and tucked the angel into her lap. Gino and Pik crouched beside her.

'Can I have a hold?' Pik asked.

'Not yet,' Jelly said. 'Maybe tomorrow. How about you and Gino get some food and blankets while I stay here with the angel?

'Why don't you go?' Gino said. 'I can stay with it. I haven't had a turn yet.'

'It doesn't want you, Gino. It only wants me. I have to stay.'

'What if I get caught?'

'Don't! And watch out for those boys.'

Gino and Pik crept out of the shed and pulled the door behind them. Jelly leaned back against the cool metal wall. She stroked the angel's hair. Its eyes closed and soon its breathing slowed. Jelly was filled with pride. The angel trusted her. This strange, wild creature trusted her enough to fall asleep in her lap. As she watched the angel sleep, a sense of calm came over her, like warm honey trickling through her bones.

She forgot, for a moment, that high school was starting in five weeks, that her parents had sold their beautiful house in the outer suburbs to buy a run-down old dump in the city so that she could go to Northbridge High. She even forgot about Stef, and the conversation where her parents had promised her she'd make new friends. Jelly was certain she'd never find a friend as good as Stef. They'd known each other since Prep.

The angel's limbs were folded loosely across her knees. Long pale lashes spread out over the crest of its cheek. Jelly picked up a clump of soft white hair. Now that it was no longer wet, when she blew gently it floated like a spider's web.

Jelly had never held anything so precious or so lovely. Looking down at the sleeping angel made her heart hurt. Even the baby birds that her dad had brought into school last year weren't as fragile as this. The enormity of what she was doing suddenly flooded through her and she remembered everything.

The next day was Christmas: Gino and Pik would

go home and then Jelly would be by herself again. Without a single friend in the world. Stef was too far away and too busy with her family to come and help her. No, Jelly needed Gino. She couldn't do this on her own. He needed to stay for the holidays. Jelly prayed for him to hurry. In her damp clothes, now that she was sitting still, she felt the cool of the night shrinking around her.

'Please,' she whispered, stroking the angel's feathers. 'Make something happen so that Gino has to stay. And Pik too, if he's allowed.' The angel stirred and a shiver passed through it like the faintest breeze.

Jelly leaned against the shed wall. Time passed. One minute, ten minutes. How long had the boys been gone? A car started up and she heard people leave a party up the road, their laughter melting into the night.

Then Jelly recognised the sound of Gino's sneakers on the concrete outside. Finally! She sat up expectantly as he opened the door. He was puffing, his hands empty. His eyes darted about. 'You gotta come,' he said. 'It's Nonna. She's in hospital!'

4

nonna

After all her complaining about her gummy knees and aching back and tired old eyes, finally it was Nonna's heart that caved in. Her heart, which Jelly thought would have been about the biggest, healthiest part of her body, stopped working right between the Christmas cake and coffee.

By the time Jelly and Gino got home the ambulance had gone, and their mums and dads with it, and only Maureen from next door was there to look after them and put baby Sophia to bed. Pik was crying in the kitchen, where all the coffee cups were half-full on the bench and the dishes still everywhere.

'Is Nonna okay?' Jelly asked, out of breath from running up the creek bank faster than she'd ever done.

'She'll be fine, honey,' Maureen said, reaching her hand out to Jelly. But Jelly didn't take it and Maureen let it drop back into her lap, her long red finger-nails clicking against each other like cicada wings. Maureen was wearing Nonna's special flowery apron. No one was allowed to wear that apron except for Nonna.

How do you know? Jelly wanted to ask. How do you know Nonna will be fine? But she didn't. She didn't feel like asking something she knew Maureen couldn't really answer.

'Well, kids, I'd say it was way past your bedtime, wouldn't you? Your mum said you'll know where the spare bedding is, Ange—'

'It's Jelly. That's what everyone calls me.'

'Right. Jelly.' Maureen tottered into the kitchen.

'Aren't they coming back tonight?' Even though Jelly was trying her best not to cry, her throat began to clog. She ran her hands briskly over her eyes to shoo away the tears.

'Not tonight,' Maureen said, stacking coffee cups

onto a tray. 'They'll need to stay with your grandma for a while.'

'Nonna,' said Jelly under her breath. Why was there a near-stranger in their house at a time like this?

Pik ran out from under the kitchen bench and into the lounge room. Jelly followed him. Gino was bunched up on the couch, tears running down his cheeks. Jelly took a sharp breath. She wouldn't cry in front of Maureen.

'What about Christmas?' Gino said, in a small voice. 'What about our presents?'

'I don't think that's the most appropriate thing to be worrying about right now,' Maureen called from the kitchen. 'Bedtime.'

Jelly, Gino and Pik trudged upstairs with a bundle of bedding in their arms. Pik was almost falling over with tiredness so Jelly tucked him in her bed, where he immediately fell asleep. She and Gino made nests on the floor. Her clothes were still damp but she couldn't face changing and doing her teeth. And there were no parents to bother them about those things anyway. She curled up in her blankets.

'Are we in trouble?' she whispered to Gino. 'Do our parents know where we were?'

'No,' said Gino. 'I mean, yes. Dad shouted at me for being out at night without asking them, but they think we were just at the playground. He would've killed me if he knew we'd taken Pik down to the creek.' He paused. 'Jelly?'

'Yeah?'

'Do you think Nonna's going to be all right?'

'Of course she will,' said Jelly, but her heart felt squeezed. 'What about the angel? We didn't leave it any food or water,' she said.

'We'll go tomorrow morning,' Gino mumbled. 'It'll be fine.'

But Jelly wasn't so sure. It was such a little thing. So small and skinny and afraid. And now she didn't know who she was more worried about: Nonna or the angel. At least Nonna had people with her. She wasn't alone.

Everything that had happened felt so mixed-up and frightening and strange, as if the world she knew had been turned upside down and shaken all about. Moving house, Nonna sick, her parents gone in the middle of the night—all of it forced its way up through Jelly's chest. And even though she squeezed her eyes shut, long silky tears streamed down her cheeks, while Gino snored in the pile of blankets next to her.

That night Jelly had the strangest dream. She dreamed she was walking along the creek with her dad as he pointed out birds. As they approached the tunnel it grew dark. Not a gentle dark like night falling but the kind where great plum-coloured clouds bloom in the sky like ink in water.

'We'd better hide in the tunnel,' said Dad. 'It looks like rain.'

But as Jelly watched, the tunnel came alive and began to transform. Its monstrous jaws opened wide. Jelly turned to her father, but he was gone. She was about to run back the way they had come when she saw something deep inside the monster's belly. It was Nonna. She was sitting in her favourite chair, smiling and beckoning. Heavy raindrops began to fall and Nonna called more impatiently for Jelly to get out of the rain. Jelly desperately wanted to go to her, but she couldn't bring herself to walk into the monster's wide, snapping jaws.

While she was deliberating, one of the cockatoos in a nearby tree swooped down and flew into the darkness. As it approached Nonna its wings grew larger and its body grew longer until soon it was a full-grown angel with long white curls that whipped about its face. Nonna reached up. The angel grasped her wrists and pulled her into the air. As they flew out of the tunnel, Nonna and the angel turned into two noisy cockatoos—flashes of white against the inky sky. When Jelly turned back to the tunnel the monster had disappeared.

christmas

Jelly woke the next morning in her grubby clothes in a twisted pile of blankets on the floor. It took her a moment to realise where she was, but then she heard Gino rustling next to her. When she sat up, she saw Pik asleep in her bed, dribbling onto her pillow. Jelly's heart sank. It was Christmas. Downstairs was a towering tree, draped in tinsel and hung with baubles. The star that Jelly had made years before sat crookedly on top. But, unless their parents had come back in the night, Jelly knew there'd be nothing under it. She couldn't imagine a worse way to wake up on

Christmas morning—Nonna in hospital, her parents gone and Maureen snoring on the couch downstairs.

Then she remembered. And despite everything, her heart leapt.

'Gino,' she whispered. 'I'm going down to see the angel. Come with me?'

'Me too,' said Pik, sitting upright, immediately awake. He jumped out of bed, onto the pile of blankets that was his brother.

'Get off.' Gino shoved him.

'I'm not taking Pik on my own,' Jelly said.

'All right, I'm coming,' Gino said. 'What about Maureen?'

'We'll leave her a note. Come on, Gino. The angel's probably starving.'

'I'm starving,' said Pik.

'You can wait.' Gino pushed him out the way as he got up.

They crept down the stairs, past Maureen who was sprawled across the couch with her eyes shut and her mouth open, even though the sunlight was slanting in through the window right over her face. The fairy lights on the Christmas tree still blinked hopefully but, as Jelly had expected, there was nothing underneath. Pik stopped to check behind the tree.

In the kitchen, Jelly found a note from her mum wedged under the biscuit tin. She must have scribbled it before they left last night.

Jelly, Dad and I have gone to the hospital with Nonna. I expect we won't be around much over the next few days, at least until we know Nonna's going to be all right. I'll need you to help Maureen with the kids. Sorry, sweetheart. We'll have an extra-special Christmas when everything is okay again. Love, Mum.

Nonna would be all right, Jelly told herself. She had to be. She went back to Pik. 'It's okay, Pikster.' She steered him into the kitchen. 'Santa's just waiting for Nonna to get better.'

They packed bread, grapes, water, bandages and other things, and the old picnic blanket from under the stairs. Jelly left a note in red texta for Maureen: *Gone to pick flowers for Nonna.* Once again her brilliant mind astonished her.

In the daylight, the tunnel seemed smaller and less frightening than the night before. Pik poked his tongue out at it as they passed. Birds swooped in and out of the peppercorn trees, squawking loudly, but the streets were quiet. Not a car or person in sight. Everyone was probably doing what people normally did on Christmas morning: sleeping in or opening presents. Not wandering the streets like orphans before the sun was fully up. They reached the mulberry tree and crawled under the fence into the school.

When Jelly opened the door to the shed, she couldn't see anything in the shadows. Then she noticed a small pile of droppings, like black pebbles. Where was the angel? Her heart lurched. She and Gino stepped into the shed, but Pik stayed outside.

'Stinks,' Gino said, wrinkling his nose. Jelly took another step forward. Suddenly there was a terrible squeal and the angel scuttled out from behind the door. Jelly fell against the side of the shed as the angel clambered up her, clawing at her T-shirt and drooling into her face. Its breath was as foul as dirty vase water.

'Get it off me! Get it *off* me!' she pleaded, her heart banging around in her chest, but Gino was laughing so hard he could barely stand up. Pik peered around the door, sniggering.

'It only wants *you*, Jelly,' Gino said. 'Not *me*. Remember?'

Jelly pulled at the angel, but it was holding on so tight its skinny fingertips were bruising her ribs. She stumbled and the angel came with her. As they landed on its injured wing, the angel bucked in pain and Jelly pulled herself free. She staggered backwards, but when she saw the angel crumple over its twisted wing she knelt down to scoop it up again.

'Stop laughing, Gino,' she said. 'It's really hurt.'

Gino crouched beside her and they studied the angel's wing as it nestled into Jelly's chest. In the daylight it was easier to see the injury. Jelly parted some feathers gently and the angel flinched. There was a small crust of dried blood matting up the downy feathers underneath and a thin white bone was sticking out of the skin, which looked puckered and pinky and sore.

'Pass me the water,' Jelly said. 'It looks like it's been bleeding in the night.'

'It needs a bang-daid,' Pik said. 'Poor angel.'

Gino and Jelly shared a furtive grin. '*Bandaid*, you idiot,' Gino said. He took the water bottle out of the plastic bag and passed it to Jelly.

'Mum says not to call me that.' Pik shuffled closer to pat the angel's head.

'You're right, Pik,' Jelly said, dribbling water over the wound. 'It does need a bandaid. But let's give it some food first.'

Pik bared his teeth at Gino.

Gino broke off a crust of bread and held it out

to the angel but it only burrowed deeper into Jelly's chest.

'You scare it. Give the bread to me.' She broke off a tiny corner and held it under the angel's nose. It sniffed, then a silvery tongue darted out and the bread was gone. 'See!' she said. But her smugness didn't last long. The angel began to cough and gag, and spat the morsel of bread out onto her lap in a gooey trail of slime. 'Ew!' She resisted the urge to push the angel off her lap. 'Did we bring any tissues?'

Gino laughed until Jelly gave him the evil eye.

As she trickled some water onto her filthy shorts to try to wash off the muck, the angel thrust its head forward and licked desperately at the wet patch.

'It's thirsty,' Pik said, gnawing on a piece of the abandoned bread stick.

Jelly tried to tip some of the water into the angel's mouth but it shied away from the bottle and would only lick it off her skin. Eventually she worked out it would drink from her cupped hands and its long tongue lapped in and out until it was full.

'Try a grape,' Gino said.

Jelly pulled one off the bunch and handed it to the angel. It sat up in her lap, suddenly interested, and sniffed at the fruit. Then it grabbed the grape in both hands and deftly peeled away the skin before popping it in its mouth.

'Ha!' Pik said. 'Monkeys do that.'

'Give it some more,' Gino said. 'It likes them.'

'Not too many,' Jelly said. 'I don't want it throwing up all over me again.'

The angel shoved the grapes into its mouth as quickly as Jelly could peel them. Gino and Pik watched, stifling fits of giggles. When they laughed the angel would hide its face against Jelly's chest and she would have to coax it out again with another peeled grape. She was beginning to feel like a mother ape.

'We'd better go soon,' said Gino, suddenly serious. 'Our parents might be back.'

'Not yet.' She stroked the angel's hair. 'We need to bandage its wing.'

Jelly pulled out some bandages and Dettol from the plastic bag and looked around the shed for something she could use as a splint. 'Get a stick from the mulberry tree,' she told Gino. 'A strong one but not too big.'

The angel lay still as Jelly bandaged its wing, like it understood she was trying to help it, and she was as gentle as she could be. Her dad had taught her how—

close to the body and folded in tight. The cockatoo had been tricky, flapping around everywhere. But the angel wasn't like that. It trusted her.

When she was finished she stroked its hair until it fell asleep. Gino sat quietly, watching. She could see that he was impressed. She was feeling quite pleased with herself, too. Perhaps she wasn't going to be an environmental scientist like her dad anymore. She might be a doctor. Or a vet. As she looked down at the sleeping angel she wondered if it was more human or more animal. It was hard to tell. It looked like a human, but it sure acted like an animal.

When Gino and Pik weren't looking, Jelly pulled its dress thing up, just a little bit, to see if it had a bottom. It did. And it looked like angels didn't wear undies.

Jelly pulled the dress down quickly before the boys saw her peeking. She didn't want to look at what it had in front. Especially if it was a boy. She wondered if all angels were that skinny or if it had been lost and hungry for a while. In the pictures she'd seen in books and churches, angels were grown-up and had long golden hair and harps and things. Or they were fat babies—cherubs, with bows and arrows. Maybe only the kid ones were this skinny? She wondered if it did have a mother and a father. Were they looking for it?

'We'll take you back,' Jelly whispered to the angel. 'Just as soon as your wing's better.'

But she wanted to show Stef first. After all, what was the point of having something magical happen to you if you couldn't share it with your best friend?

Gino was pulling bark off a mulberry twig. 'Can we go now?' he said. 'Dad'll kill me if we're not there when they get back. I'm supposed to wash his car today as punishment for staying out last night.'

'That's so mean,' said Jelly. 'It's Christmas Day!'

Gino shrugged. 'Yeah.'

Jelly stroked the angel's wings and felt all her anger towards her uncle come up out of her chest, like a gust of hot air, and rush down her arms and through her fingertips. The angel stirred and then settled again. 'Let's go then,' she said, and took Pik's hand. Gino pulled the door shut behind them and slid the bolt across.

'It's not going anywhere,' Jelly said.

'It can still crawl,' Gino said. 'It might get out. I don't want it to escape.'

'What do you mean you don't want it to escape? It's not like it belongs to you.'

'Yes, it does,' Gino said. 'I found it.'

'*What*?'

'In the creek. I was the first to see it. You didn't even want to go into the water.'

'But *I'm* the one looking after it. It wants *me*.'

'Yeah, Gino,' Pik piped up from behind Jelly's legs. 'Jelly fixed its wing.'

'Shut up, Pik! This has nothing to do with you. It's my angel. I'm taking it home with me to show my friends.'

'You can't do that,' Jelly said.

'Why not?'

'Because, because…the adults might see it. You can't just show it to anybody.'

'I bet you want to show it to *your* friends. Why can't I show mine?'

Jelly felt her cheeks heat up. 'That's not the same. Your friends are…'

'What?'

'They're boys! They'll hurt it, or something, Gino. Don't be stupid!'

Gino's face flared red. 'I'm not stupid. You're stupid. I can do what I want. And anyway, *finders keepers*.'

Jelly glared at Gino and he glared back. A moth

39

of panic banged around in her chest. Gino couldn't keep the angel. He couldn't. Even if he was the first to see it. That didn't mean anything. It wanted *her*. She was the one looking after it. It was hers, not Gino's.

All the way back to her house Gino walked ahead of Jelly, and Pik skipped to keep up. They didn't speak to each other once.

6

a silver heart

'Shhh,' Maureen said as they came in the back door,
even though they hadn't actually said anything yet.
She was sitting on the couch with Sophia, watching
cartoons with the sound down low. 'Your mum and
dad are home, Jelly. They're asleep upstairs.'

'How's Nonna?' Jelly asked.

'They're just keeping an eye on her for now,
honey.'

'Where are my parents?' Gino asked.

'Well,' said Maureen, turning to face him. 'The
strangest thing just happened. That old gum tree out

the front dropped an enormous branch onto your dad's car. Almost flattened it. That tree's been there for almost thirty years and never lost a twig.'

'Not the Alfa!'

Maureen nodded.

'Dad's going to be *so* mad. Where is he?'

'Gone with the tow truck. They'll be lucky to find a garage open on Christmas Day, though.' Maureen grinned. 'Looks like you're stuck here for a while, I'd say.'

'I'm going upstairs,' Jelly said, stifling a smile. Her uncle was obsessed with his new car. Sometimes she thought he cared more about it than Gino, Pik or Sophia. Serves him right, she thought.

Jelly didn't go into her room straight away. Instead she stood in the doorway of her parents' room and watched her mum and dad. Her dad was frowning in his sleep. She couldn't imagine why anyone would want to grow up. All those things that adults had to worry about. And all that sitting around talk, talk, talking when there were so many trees to climb and gardens to explore. She thought about this as she listened to her mum's quiet, feathery breath and her dad's snorkling one. After a while she wandered into the study to look up angels on the internet.

The first site she found was full of paintings of angels. None of them looked like hers. These angels were tall and graceful, and floating on clouds, with harps or doves in their hands. Also they all looked very human. Jelly's angel was much more like a creature, wilder and more animal-like. Jelly hadn't seen it fly, obviously, but it didn't even seem to be able to walk on two legs. It mostly scuttled crab-like across the floor. The only thing it had in common with these angels was its face, its delicate porcelain features.

Jelly typed in 'can angels come to earth?' and found many stories of people who'd seen angels. But in all the cases, angels had come to them, not the other way around. No one had ever just stumbled across an angel in the wild. This made her wonder: had their angel been on its way somewhere when it got caught up in the creek rubbish? She turned the computer off.

In her bedroom, Jelly curled up on the lumpy blankets that she and Gino had slept in. She watched the shadows of the peppercorn trees on the ceiling, and thought about the angel. She wasn't going to let Gino take it home. It was too dangerous. And Gino lived too far away to be able to get it back to the creek. No, Gino was wrong. She would have to show him somehow. He used to listen to her. Why had he suddenly become so difficult?

And he was so mean to Pik. He sounded just like his dad when he bullied Pik. Except Gino never said anything when his dad got stuck into him, just stood there, eyes glassed over, like a rabbit caught in the headlights of a car.

It drove Jelly crazy. She couldn't imagine ever being scared of her parents the way Gino seemed to be scared of his. Now that his precious car was dented, Zio Mario would be in a foul mood. And Gino would be the one to cop it. She almost felt sorry for him then.

Jelly rolled over onto her side and glimpsed a small pile of badly wrapped presents hidden under her bed. She smiled. They were obviously Gino's. He was terrible at gift-wrapping.

She pulled one out and saw her name on it in fat black texta. Of all the presents hidden under there, she had pulled out hers. That was a sign, she decided. It wouldn't hurt to take a little peek. It was probably something awful anyway, like the stinky perfume he'd given her from the two-dollar shop. Or the ugly shell paperweight he had made at school. Jelly giggled. A little peek would prepare her for the worst. But when she saw what was inside she gasped.

It was a silver heart locket. The one she had seen last Christmas and had so desperately wanted. She had told Gino that all her friends had them, but her parents had said no. Gino must have remembered.

Jelly suddenly felt very bad. Not just for peeking at her present but also for fighting with Gino. It had been a pretty ordinary Christmas for all of them. But at least she was in her own house. It must be much worse for him. She wrapped the locket up again, slipped it back in among the others, and decided to risk a truce. She crept down the stairs.

'Psst, Gino,' she hissed, while Pik was distracted by the cartoons. 'Want to come outside?'

'Okay.' Gino slid off the couch and followed her to the back door. Jelly wasn't sure if she had been forgiven or if she was just the best option he had at that moment, but she had to admit that was one of the best things about Gino. He didn't stay mad for long.

7

the bullies

Jelly and Gino climbed the apricot tree, searching for fruit that hadn't been pecked by the birds. The good apricots were high up, near where the branches became too thin to hold them. From there they could see over the back fence, over the creek, as far as the school.

Neither of them mentioned the angel but Jelly knew they were both thinking about it. She hoped it wasn't too hot in the shed. There was a breeze at the top of the tree but Jelly was still sticky with sweat and apricot juice. Above them fine clouds like fairy floss scudded across the sky. The heat pressed down on their scalps and turned their faces pink. Gino threw an apricot stone into the vegetable garden in front of Nonna's flat.

'Careful,' Jelly said. 'Nonna will kill you if you touch her tomatoes.'

Gino grinned, then his face fell. 'Nonna's not going to die, is she?' he asked in a small voice.

'Of course not,' Jelly said, but she heard the hesitation in her voice. The thought made her sick. She couldn't imagine what it would be like if her grandmother was gone. Nonna had lived with them since Jelly was small. Since her nonno had died. Every day after school it was nonna who listened to all the intricate details of Jelly's day: who was fighting, which girl had the nicest hair, which boys had been particularly annoying or smelly.

Gino spat out an apricot stone and sighed. 'I wish you had a pool.'

'Me too.'

'Can you swim in the creek?'

'Yuck,' Jelly said. 'Don't think so. We could dunk our feet though.'

'Good idea,' said Gino, and without another word they were out of the tree and over the fence.

It was much cooler by the water. Jelly and Gino

waded in the shallows and watched insects skitter across the glossy mud. In the tunnel, two boys were throwing stones into the water.

'They're the boys who rode past last night.' Jelly frowned. 'They're always in the tunnel.'

'From your new high school?'

'Yeah.'

She watched as one of the boys picked up a big stone and hurled it at a duck, missing it by only a few centimetres. The boys laughed as the duck paddled away, quacking indignantly.

'They shouldn't do that,' Jelly muttered.

'Why don't you tell them?' Gino grinned. 'Go on, I dare you.'

Jelly faced him. She knew it was a stupid dare but she couldn't resist the opportunity to impress Gino. 'All right. I will then.'

'I was *joking*.'

'Just watch me.'

Jelly strode towards the tunnel trying to hide her nerves. Even though she had seen the boys around the creek most days she had never been this close to them and had certainly never spoken to them. One of the boys was tall and lanky with a face like a pepperoni pizza. The other was short and stocky and looked like he hadn't evolved much from his caveman ancestors. Both of them glared at Jelly as she entered the tunnel. Part of her, the sensible part, told her she should just keep walking—right through the tunnel and out the other side. Gino wouldn't think any less of her. But the other part of her felt angry. Angry enough to say something without thinking of the consequences.

She heard her voice come out smaller than she had hoped. 'You shouldn't throw stones at those ducks. You might hurt them.'

Neanderthal Boy snorted.

'So?' said Pizza Face.

'So…just that. You should leave them alone. They haven't done anything to you.'

Pizza Face's eyes narrowed. 'Who says?'

'Yeah, who says?' Neanderthal Boy chuckled.

Jelly chewed her lip while she considered her next move. Going back the way she came was looking like the best option. Walking straight ahead would require more confidence than her quaking legs could muster. Another boy appeared at the other end of the tunnel. A boy she hadn't seen before. He stood against the light that streamed in from the entrance. Jelly couldn't make out his face, but he was tall with straight black hair that hung down to his shoulders. Now she knew she was beaten. There was no way she was going to stand up to a whole gang of boys just to save a bunch of ducks. If only Stef was there. Stef would have the perfect comeback line to flatten them. She always did. Stef was bold and brave. Not like Gino, who was fidgeting in the shade of the willow trees.

The new boy called out. 'Jack! Budgie! You coming or what?'

So now she knew their names. Jack, the pizza face, and Budgie, the Neanderthal. They turned. Then they headed off in the direction of the new boy without giving her a second glance. Jelly watched them disappear.

She turned to Gino, who was gaping at her. From where he stood, he wouldn't have seen the third boy appear. Or heard what had been said. It would have looked as if Jelly had shooed Jack and Budgie away like two annoying flies. Jelly grinned and made a gesture like she was brushing dust off her shoulders. She loved impressing Gino.

Jelly sauntered back to the shade. 'Easy as.' She grinned. 'Guys who pick on ducks are wimps.' She was happy to bathe in Gino's admiration while it lasted. And then, feeling like she might have control over the situation again, she said, 'I reckon we should check up on the angel. Let's take it some more food.' Jelly patted her pockets, which bulged with apricots.

It wasn't until they had rounded the corner of the school that Jelly heard the ominous swish of bike wheels behind them. She turned. Jack and Budgie and the new boy were heading towards them. Jelly pulled Gino under the cover of the mulberry tree but it was no use, they had already been spotted. Jack hoicked his bike onto the footpath and braked in front of them, blocking their way. Budgie and the other boy rode in circles around the street.

'Oh, look, it's the duck-saver,' Jack said. 'Not thinking of going into the school, are you? It's out of bounds over the holidays.'

'I *guessed* that,' Jelly said. 'It's locked anyway.'

A smile spread over Jack's face and he jumped off his bike. It clattered onto the footpath.

'Who's talking about locks? You weren't thinking of getting in under the fence, were you? 'Cause that's not allowed.' He brought his sweaty, pimply face close to Jelly's. 'And they're not school rules, they're *my* rules. You hear?'

The other two boys pulled up behind Jack. Jelly

looked at Gino for support, but he was staring at the dirty marks on his sneakers like they were the most fascinating thing he'd ever seen.

She stared right back at Jack—he sure was ugly up close—and said, 'Why would I want to go to school on the *holidays*?'

She was thinking this was a pretty good come-back considering the circumstances, and was thrilled to hear the new boy laugh.

Jack glared at him. 'What's so funny, loser?'

'She's right, Jack.' The boy shrugged. 'Why would you want to hang around school on the holidays? Come on, Budgie, let's go.' He flicked his long black fringe out of his eyes and shot Jelly a grin before he and Budgie wheeled off down the street.

Jack scrambled to follow them.

Jelly watched them go. Mainly to make sure they were out of sight before she and Gino sneaked into the school, but also because that new kid made her curious.

She turned to Gino. He had that scared, tight-mouthed face on him, like when his dad shouted at him. Jelly had no idea how he was going to survive high school in a year's time.

'Hey, Gino,' she said, 'who does this remind you

of?' She crossed her eyes and pushed her eyebrows down her forehead.

Gino laughed. 'How about this?' He shoved his tongue into his bottom lip and pulled out his ears.

'You just need the pimples,' Jelly giggled, squashing a ripe mulberry onto his face.

'Hey!' Gino yelled, but Jelly had already slipped through the fence to the other side.

8

trapped

The tin shed was as hot as an oven, and the angel didn't get up when they walked in. It slid its eyes over to them, then down to the floor. It lay on the blanket, breathing fast, knees tucked up under its chin. It had become so pale it was almost translucent and its ribs were poking through its skin.

'It doesn't look so good,' Jelly said, her stomach tightening.

'It's fine,' said Gino. 'Just hot, that's all.' But he looked as worried as she felt. Looking after an angel was turning out to be nothing like looking after a bird.

She crouched by the angel and tipped some water into her hands. The water was warm, but the angel lapped at it. She dribbled the last of it on the back of the angel's neck, where its fairy-floss hair was matted with sweat. 'Can you fill this up?' She held out the water bottle to Gino.

'What did your last slave die of?'

'Very funny,' she said. But she didn't want to get into another fight with him just when they were getting along again.

Jelly left the door open to let some air in, though there wasn't much of a breeze. A tin shed on a hot day was probably the worst place they could have chosen to keep the angel, but it was too dangerous to move it in the daylight. Especially with those boys hanging around.

She filled up the bottle at the bubblers behind the school building. From where she stood she could see through the glass doors, down the main hallway. It reminded her of her own primary school. The long corridor, with the library at the end. Ms Stevenson-Brown had filled the library with beanbags and posters. It even had an old window display dummy, which they were allowed to dress in funny outfits that she kept in a box behind her desk.

Jelly remembered the lunchtime that she and Stef had put every single item of clothing on the dummy, including thirteen hats and seven pairs of glasses. They had laughed so hard she thought her sides would split. Ms Stevenson-Brown had just smiled at them as she reshelved the books.

High school teachers weren't like that. Courtney Wilcox, whose brother went to Northbridge High, said that if you were late or brought the wrong book to class you got a detention. Just like that. Jelly could barely remember which books belonged to which subject let alone which day she needed to bring them. And Northbridge High was so big it was like a city. How was she ever going to find her way around?

When she had picked up the brown paper packages full of shiny new textbooks and sharp pencils and strange mathematical plastic things and calculators with numbers she didn't recognise, she felt sick.

If only she had even just one friend starting with her. Everyone would already have their friends from primary school and all the groups would be as good as closed. Jelly would be the only one left over. Not for the first time she wished she was going to the same school as Stef, but she knew, even without asking her parents, that they would never have been able to afford a private school. Northbridge High had been the next best option.

Jelly drank from the bubblers, washed her sticky hands and slicked back her hair. She prepared herself to make the dash across the searing courtyard when she saw something out of the corner of her eye. She paused. Someone was by the fence. She ducked behind the building but even before he called out she knew she had been spotted. Jack.

'Oi, you!' She could hear in his voice that he was half furious that she'd disobeyed him and half thrilled that he would now have an excuse to punish her.

Jelly flattened herself against the bricks, heart racing, and cursed herself for confronting him under the bridge. She had now officially made her first enemy. Even before she had made a friend. Brilliant.

Then, in the gentlest puff of breeze, Jelly saw the shed door sway. She'd left it open! There was no way she could let Jack into the school.

She raced across the hot concrete. 'Just getting some water from the bubblers, Jack,' she called loudly so that Gino would figure out what was happening and stay hidden.

When she got to him, she could see that he was deciding how to best manage her waywardness. She leaned down to peel back the fence but he pinned the wire to the ground with his big, boofy sneaker.

'If you like school so much,' he sneered, 'you can stay there.'

It was so hot and her head was so fried and she was feeling so sick about Jack discovering her angel coiled up in the shed that all Jelly could do was gawp at him like a mute fish.

'Very funny, Jack.' Her voice was more desperate than she would have liked. 'Let me out. I told you I was just getting a drink.'

'Why should I? You can stay in there all summer as far as I'm concerned.'

She watched as he snapped a branch off the mulberry tree. Then he began to thread the stick through the fence, so that it would hold the wire in place.

Budgie and the new boy rode up behind Jack onto the footpath and watched curiously. Jack didn't look up from his work. All the same when Jelly saw the dark-haired boy she felt a glimmer of hope.

'What are you doing?' the new boy asked, speaking to Jack but looking at Jelly. The soles of Jelly's feet were burning up and she knew they would blister in the days to come.

'Trapping me in the school,' she answered, rolling her eyes as if she didn't care.

'There,' Jack said, standing back to admire his work. He smiled, pleased with himself. Jelly had to admit he'd done a good job. There was no way she could pull the stick out from her side.

The heat on the soles of her feet forced her to the shade of the tree. 'There you go,' Jack chuckled. 'You've got mulberry leaves and water. That should be plenty to keep a little worm like you going over summer.' He turned to give Budgie a high five but his friend wasn't ready so Jack dropped his hand awkwardly by his side. Budgie and the new boy watched Jelly but whatever happened she wouldn't cry. She'd never give Jack the satisfaction. Besides, Gino was in the shed, so she wasn't in it alone. And, most importantly, the angel was safe.

'Let's go,' Jack said, swinging his gangly leg over his bike. Budgie followed, but the new boy hesitated. 'I'm heading down to the creek for a bit,' he called out. 'Catch you guys later.' Then he glided off in the other direction. When Jack and Budgie were out of sight, he looped back.

From her place in the shade, Jelly watched him untwist the wood from the wire fence. He had long brown fingers with grubby bitten nails. Around one wrist he wore a leather bracelet threaded with multi-coloured beads. Jelly had never seen a boy wear a bracelet before.

Once he had the wood out, the boy lifted up the wire. Jelly slid under, trying to avoid taking the scabs off her knees again.

'What did you do that for?' she said, when she was through. 'If Jack finds out he'll kill you.'

The boy shrugged. 'Maybe 'cause it's Christmas?' He smiled, then got back on his bike. 'Where'd you leave your shoes?'

'By the creek.'

He looked at the white-hot pavement, then at Jelly crouching in the shade. 'Wanna dink?'

'Thanks,' she said. Then loudly for Gino's benefit, 'A ride home'd be great.'

Gino wasn't necessarily school-smart, as his father liked to remind him, but he was smart in other ways and Jelly knew he would have been listening care-fully. He would have understood what was going on.

So she swung up behind the boy with the black hair and the brown arms, and he took her all the way back to the creek without saying a word. As they coasted down St Peter's Road, Jelly couldn't help wondering what Stef would think if she saw her now, on the back of a boy's bike with the wind in her hair.

They arrived at the creek and the boy pulled up in the shade of a peppercorn tree. Jelly clambered awkwardly off the bike. When she turned around to thank him he was gone.

Jelly collected her shoes and Gino's from the muddy creek bank. She could see Gino in the distance making his way home over the bridge. She climbed the apricot tree to watch out for him, and thought about that boy. How lucky they were he'd turned up from nowhere. And she realised she hadn't even asked him his name.

9

keeping secrets

Jelly and Gino peered though the back window. Only Jelly's mum was in the kitchen. Gino's dad wasn't in sight. He breathed a sigh of relief and wiped the sweat from his top lip.

'Mum won't say anything,' Jelly assured him. 'She's fine with me playing by the creek.' She grabbed Gino's hand and pulled him through the back door. They tried to slip past Jelly's mother but she grabbed Jelly's arm before they could get away. 'Uh-uh. Straight up to the shower, you two.' She rolled her eyes. 'Don't think I don't know where you've been.

You'd better get cleaned up before your parents get home, Gino.'

Jelly washed and changed into fresh clothes, then waited for Gino in her room. Her dad walked past and blew Jelly a kiss. 'How's Nonna?' she asked.

'All right.' He smiled. 'Making trouble as usual.'

But Jelly saw the sadness flicker over his face. Her stomach clenched into a fist. Was anyone telling them the truth? Jelly was desperate to see Nonna for herself.

'Can I visit her, Dad?'

'Not just yet, sweetheart.'

At last Gino came out of the bathroom. Jelly beckoned him into her room. 'How was the angel?' she whispered. 'Did you get it to eat anything?'

'I tried to feed it some apricots but it wouldn't let me near it so I left them on the rug. I filled a tray of water for it, though.'

'Good thinking. Imagine if Jack found it.'

'Lunch,' her mum called.

Zio Mario was back and in a foul mood. You'd think it was *his* mum who was in the hospital from all the fuss that Zia Pia was making over him. He strode over to the table and waited to be waited on. Jelly and Gino sat as far away from him as possible and

63

far from Sophia, who dribbled and threw her food around. Somebody had put Nonna's special chair by the back window, as if it was watching out for her to come home.

It wasn't a real Christmas lunch; everything felt strange without Nonna around. They sat in silence. Partly because of Nonna and partly because no one felt like coaxing Zio Mario out of his dark mood. Jelly's mum dished up the pasta left over from the night before and Jelly and Gino wolfed down two servings each without looking up from their plates. Pik, as usual, just picked at his food, which was partly how he got his name, and also because it was short for *piccolo*, which means small.

All the kids had been given nicknames when they were little, but Pik's and Jelly's were the only ones that had stuck. Jelly was short for her full name, which was long and old-fashioned and had never felt like it belonged only to her.

After moving his lasagne round his plate for a while, Pik suddenly announced to everyone at the table, 'We found an angel.'

Jelly looked up as Gino choked on his garlic bread. He coughed then gave Pik the greasiest look she'd seen in a long time. Jelly, her heart hammering in her chest, stared at her parents, waiting to see what they would say.

'That's nice,' said Mum, helping herself to the *zeppole*.

Jelly breathed out.

'It's true,' Pik said, ignoring Gino and pushing away the forkful of lasagne Zia Pia was trying to sneak into his mouth. 'We found it in the creek. Last night.'

'You kids haven't been taking Pik down to the creek, have you?' Zia Pia said. 'You know he can't swim. And there was that boy who drowned—'

'Jelly's not going to let them go near the water,' Jelly's mum interrupted. 'They're perfectly safe—'

'I'm not having my kids wandering down by the creek—'

'Pik's just making up stories,' said Gino. 'Aren't you, Pik?' Then he hissed, 'Just like a kid who wants to stay with his baby sister would.'

Pik's face crumpled and he looked down at his plate. 'Anyway,' he said quietly, to no one in particular. 'I drew it a picture. Father Christmas and his goats.'

Gino snorted. 'Reindeer, dummy. They're not goats. And anyway, there's no such thing as Father Christmas.'

'*Gino*,' Zio Mario warned.

'It's true,' Gino sulked. 'And he knows it, too.'

'If Pik wants to believe in Father Christmas or angels or anything else for that matter, you shouldn't spoil it for him,' Zia Pia scolded, wiping Sophia's mouth with a cloth.

'Some Christmas,' Gino muttered under his breath.

'Don't think I didn't hear that, Gino.' His dad's face darkened. 'What, you think this is all about you? With your nonna in the hospital and your mum worried sick—'

'Hey,' Jelly's dad said gently. 'It's been a hard time for all of us. And Gino's right. It's not been much of a Christmas. Especially for the kids.'

Jelly gave her dad a grateful smile but Gino just picked at the tablecloth, his face dark and brooding.

10

the broken wing

After coffee, everyone vanished. The house was instantly quiet. Jelly, Gino and Pik slipped out the back door.

'Are we going to see the angel?' Pik said, bouncing alongside them. 'Are we? Are we?'

'Shut up, Pik,' Gino snapped. 'You're lucky you're even coming with us after what you said at lunch.'

'Give him a break,' Jelly said. 'It's not like they believed him.'

Gino glared at them and marched ahead.

On Ivy Street there was no one around. They

heard the crack of a ball against a cricket bat then hoots of laughter coming from someone's backyard. Other houses let out the steady drone of overworked air conditioners. Jelly pictured kids playing with their Christmas presents and parents stuffed like turkeys, snoozing on couches. That was what her family would usually be doing.

They slipped under the fence and dashed across the blazing schoolyard. Gino pushed open the door and a blast of heat emptied from the shed.

'Yuck,' said Pik. 'I'm not going in there.'

'Oh, the poor angel,' Jelly said.

Gino and Jelly tiptoed into the stuffy darkness, to the corner where the angel was lying like a crumpled mat.

Jelly crouched beside it. The angel was panting shallowly. She placed her hand on its clammy fore-head, but it didn't open its eyes this time. A sour milky smell hovered around it. One wing was spread out across the floor, the other one, the bandaged one, was tucked in tight along the angel's spine. A dirty yellow liquid was oozing from a dark patch of dried blood. The sour smell was coming from its wound. She pulled out a strawberry from her pocket and held it under the angel's nose. It didn't stir.

'We have to do something. I think its wing might be infected.'

Gino leaned in to look, but jerked back when the smell hit his nostrils.

'Poor angel.' Pik was still standing by the doorway and his voice was small and frightened. 'We should take it to the creek to cool it down.'

'We're not taking it to the creek,' Gino snapped.

'It's a good idea, Gino,' Jelly said.

'What? And let it go?'

'No, just cool it down. Look at it. It's too hot in here.'

'We can tip water on it.'

'That won't be enough.'

'You have to do what Jelly says, Gino.' Pik was almost crying.

'It's none of your business, Pik.' Gino turned to Jelly, lips tight. 'How would we get it there, anyway? Without anyone seeing?'

'Sophia's pram,' Pik suggested. 'We could hide it in there.'

'Good thinking, Pikster.' Jelly grinned at him.

Gino frowned. 'Suppose you're going to send me back to get it?'

'No, we should stick together in case those boys

are around.' She touched the angel's hair.

'Don't worry, little angel,' Pik called as they backed out of the shed. 'We'll be back soon.'

The house was still quiet when they got back, but even so Jelly tiptoed upstairs to see who was home. Her dad was in the study, eyes glued to the computer screen and his bird thesis spread out all around him. Sophia was sleeping in a cot next to him. Jelly tugged one of her sunhats off the back of the door, shoved it under her T-shirt, then tiptoed out of the room.

'Jelly?' her dad whispered, as she reached the landing.

Jelly froze. Did her dad know they were up to something? She turned around slowly.

'I almost forgot. Stef called.'

Jelly's heart soared.

'She wanted to wish you a happy Christmas. I said I'd get you to call back.'

Jelly was torn. She desperately wanted to talk to her best friend. She had so much to tell her. And it felt like days since they'd spoken. But Pik and Gino were waiting downstairs and the angel was baking in the shed.

'I'll call her tonight.'

'Really?' her dad said. 'You're always complaining that you can't get onto her.'

'Gino and Pik are waiting for me. I have to go.'

Jelly's dad shrugged. 'I'm glad you kids are getting along so well. I thought you'd gone off Gino a bit.'

'Nah,' said Jelly. 'He's okay.' She scooted back downstairs.

Gino had already brought Sophia's pram around the back and Pik was almost wetting himself with excitement.

'Shh, Pik, you'll get us busted.' Jelly tossed the sunhat into the pram. 'We'll have to go the long way round. There's no way we'd get the pram over the back fence.'

The old lady from across the road was sitting in the shade of her front porch as they passed. She was fanning herself with junk mail. '*Buon Natale!*' she called out, waving so that the pale flesh underneath her fat arms jiggled.

'Merry Christmas,' Jelly called back, without slowing down.

'You taking your baby sister for a walk?'

'Yep.'

'Good children.'

Jelly giggled. Even Gino couldn't hide a grin.

At the hole in the fence, Jelly told Gino and Pik to wait with the pram while she fetched the angel.

'Hurry,' said Gino. 'I don't want those boys catching me here. Especially with a *pram*.'

Inside the shed it smelled even worse than before. Jelly breathed through her mouth. The air was hot and dry. 'Hey, little angel,' she cooed, approaching slowly. It didn't stir.

Jelly had brought one of Sophia's blankets with her. She tucked one side under the angel's limp body and rolled it onto the blanket, folding in its good wing first. Gently she lifted the injured wing. It dangled loosely in her hand. The angel didn't even flinch. Jelly leaned in close to its face, her heart beating fast. Then she heard them. Little raspy puffs like the swish of a skirt on dry grass. The angel was still breathing. She exhaled and picked it up carefully, holding it close to her chest. One of the angel's eyelids floated open and its pale eye rolled back. It let out a tiny sigh.

'I'm so sorry, little one,' she said, tears pricking at her eyes. 'We're taking you to the creek to cool down.'

Jelly carried the angel to the fence. Pik was squashing mulberries with his foot and Gino's hands were slammed into his pockets, his shoulders stiff as he looked up and down the street. He lifted the fence and Jelly slid the bundle to them, then slipped through.

Pik crouched by the motionless angel. 'Is it dead?' he asked in dismay.

'It's fine,' Gino said, looking at Jelly for confirmation.

'Yeah, it's fine, Pik.' But worry was flooding through her. Jelly folded the angel into the cramped space of the pram. She pulled the blanket up and placed the sunhat over its pale face. The angel didn't make a sound.

They pushed the pram along the street. Above them the sky was as white as bones. A tram clattered past but otherwise the street was empty. All the same, Jelly kept a lookout for Jack and Budgie and the other boy. She didn't know what they'd do if they ran into them.

Finally, they made it to the creek. The angel opened its eyes and lifted its head a little to sniff at the air.

Gino pulled a rope from his pocket.

'What's that?' Jelly asked.

'You don't want it to get away, do you?' he mumbled, his cheeks flushing.

Pik and Jelly watched, open-mouthed, as he tied the rope around the angel's ankle.

'Not too tight,' Pik said softly. 'You'll hurt it.'

Gino glared at him. When he was done, he looked at Jelly, challenging her to question him. Jelly turned away, pushing down her anger. It wasn't worth the fight. She had got Gino to agree to bring the angel to the creek; that was all that mattered for now.

Jelly slipped off her sneakers and lifted the angel out of the pram. Its body lay limp but a thin hand slid out from the folds of the blanket and grasped her wrist. She carried the angel to the water. Gino walked alongside her, the end of the rope in his hand.

When Jelly reached the milky edge she knelt in the mud and gently rolled the angel into the creek, supporting it under its arms. At first the angel drifted to the bottom, its feet and the tip of its wing sinking into the mud. But then she felt a jolt through its body, and the hand around her wrist sprang open. A sound like the wheeze of an old accordion burst from its chest and the angel's eyes floated shut.

Jelly took one hand out from under its sharp shoulder blades and scooped water onto its hair. Gritty water ran into the hollows of the angel's face. Its silver tongue darted out to catch a trickle rolling down its cheek. As she watched, the angel opened its eyes, bright now, and stared up into hers. Jelly thought she glimpsed a smile flickering across its face. She smiled back. The angel's eyes didn't leave hers for a moment.

Jelly stayed still, listening to the creek: the insects buzzing, water rushing, willows whispering. The angel's good wing slowly unfurled and floated to the surface. Even the broken wing seemed to uncrumple and the gummy bandage was washed clean. Gino squatted on one side of her, holding on tight to the rope, while Pik lay on her other side, looking up into the clouds and humming to himself.

After a while Jelly felt Gino tugging at the rope. 'We'd better head back.'

'We haven't been very long,' Jelly said.

'Sophia might need the pram.'

Jelly frowned and stroked the feathers on the angel's good wing. She felt her irritation towards Gino flare up. 'We always need to get back for something. I wish we could stay longer for once. Stupid Sophia. I wish she wasn't around.'

'Don't wish that!'

'Why not?' Jelly said. 'She's annoying. Don't pretend you don't think so, too.'

'She's my *sister*. Don't say things like that!'

Gino's reaction surprised Jelly. Usually he was the first one to get stuck into his siblings. Why was he defending his sister now?

'All right,' she said, kicking a stone into the water. 'We'll take it back to that horrible hot old shed then.'

Jelly leaned forward to hitch the angel up under its arms. That was when she noticed. A group of brown speckled ducks was swimming towards them from the tunnel, slowly at first, but then paddling faster and faster. The angel twitched. A low whine came from the back of its throat and its head jerked from side to side. As the ducks scrambled for the bank, the angel began to moan. Jelly looked down to see what was wrong. She looked back at the tunnel and that was when she saw it: a flash as bright as lightning. It came and went so quickly that at first Jelly thought it was sunlight glinting off the water. But then, spilling out from the tunnel, came the strangest thing she'd ever seen. A long flat wave was rolling towards them, gaining speed as it approached. And, as if this wasn't strange enough, the wave was moving *against* the current. The creek was flowing away from them but the wave was coming towards them. As it got closer the angel howled and jerked against the rope.

'Get it out!' Gino yelled, holding on tight.

Jelly grabbed the angel's slippery arms and pulled it out of the water. Pik clambered to his feet and ducked behind a tree. The wave reared up as it passed them, frothing and milky brown, almost reaching out for them. Jelly scrambled up the bank, dragging the angel with her. It squealed loudly and arched its neck towards the water, arms flailing. Gino went to help Jelly and they carried the squirming angel to the pram. It hissed and lashed out with its bony fingers, but they wrestled it into the pram and finally it lay still, only its eyes rolling about. Jelly wrapped it tightly in the blanket and Gino buckled it in.

They looked back. The water was calm again.

'What *was* that?' Gino's eyes were wild.

'Looked like a tsunami,' Jelly said, her heart in her mouth.

'In a *creek*?'

'Well, *I* don't know.'

'Oh, man, that was weird.'

They looked at the angel. It was curled up tight, but its eyes darted from side to side. As Jelly leaned in to pull the blanket up, the angel clutched her wrist with its scrawny hand.

She jumped. 'Oh, it scared me!'

The angel's lips opened and closed, but no sound came out.

'What is it?' she said. 'Gino, look. I think it's trying to talk.' But when the angel saw Gino, it snapped its mouth shut and turned its head to the side.

'I didn't see anything.'

'It was before.'

They watched the angel for a while but it lay still.

'Maybe I was wrong,' Jelly said.

They pushed the pram to the school, all of them lost in their separate thoughts. The angel didn't stir.

At the fence Gino and Pik left to take the pram back before anyone missed it and Jelly carried the angel to the shed. It was still hot inside but at least the angel felt cool. She laid it down on the old grey blanket and whispered in its ear. 'What *was* that in the creek, little one? Was it coming for you?'

But the angel rolled away from her and curled into a ball. Jelly stroked its hair and blew on the back of its neck. Soon its eyes drifted closed and its breathing slowed. She waited until she was sure it was asleep then tiptoed out of the shed. Already the sun had shifted lower in the sky. Even though the heat made her head pound, Jelly ran all the way home.

11

the storm

That night the bad things started to happen.

Jelly was nearly asleep when a storm rolled into the neighbourhood. Usually thunder didn't scare her but this was so loud it shook their house like it was made of paper. Jelly lay awake and rigid in her bed. Gino and Pik were asleep on the floor.

There was another mighty clap of thunder and at the same time a flash of lightning flooded the room. Normally, Jelly counted the seconds between the two to see how far away the storm was, but this time the sound and the light appeared at exactly the same moment. The closeness of the storm made her skin crawl.

Jelly kicked off the sheet and stepped over Pik's sleeping body to get to the window. She pulled back the blind. Another flash of lightning struck and it was as if the electricity shot right through her, entering through her eye sockets and exiting through her toes. She stumbled backwards, blinded, and fell over Pik onto her bed. When she opened her eyes her vision was gone and pain split through her head like an axe.

'Mum!' she screamed. 'Dad! I can't see!'

By the time everyone in the house had been woken, Jelly's vision had returned and she had an almighty headache.

'Migraine,' her parents concluded.

'I had them as a teenager, too,' her mum said, dampening Jelly's forehead with a cool washcloth. 'It's hormonal, I'm afraid.'

'But I'm only twelve!'

'You're half-Italian,' Zia said, smiling. 'Italian girls mature early. You'll most likely get your women's business soon. That's exciting, isn't it, love?'

Gino made a face like he was dry-retching and Jelly squirmed.

'Get Jel a glass of water, Gino,' Mum sighed.

'What business?' said Pik, jumping up and down on her bed. 'Will I have business, too?'

And even though a herd of elephants were pounding through her head Jelly couldn't help but laugh. 'No, Pik,' she said. 'You can't have everything.'

Outside, thunder and lightning were still crashing around and a howling wind rattled the windows. Great silver ropes of rain lashed at the glass.

'Well, it never rains but it pours,' joked Jelly's dad.

'Everyone back to sleep now,' her mum said. 'Everything will be better tomorrow, I'm sure.'

But she was wrong. Very wrong.

12

finders keepers

That night Jelly's dreams were filled with angels. She recognised the big one from her dream the night before. It was flashing in and out of the storm clouds as bright as lightning. Each time it swept over Jelly's house its mouth opened wide and ground-shaking thunder rolled out. Jelly and the baby angel huddled in the little tin shed, sheltering from the storm. Rain pelted the tin roof and streams of water ran down the leaky walls. Jelly felt water begin to puddle at her feet. She looked up at the ceiling but couldn't see where the rain was getting in. Then she turned. The baby angel was crouched silently beside her, mouth wide, rain pouring from its eyes in a river of tears.

When Jelly woke, Gino and Pik were still asleep on her floor, but she could hear someone moving around downstairs. She lifted her head slowly from her pillow and was relieved to find that her headache had disappeared along with the storm. Remnants of her dream hung around her like cloud vapour. She thought of Nonna waking up all alone in the hospital and then of her angel in the little shed. She needed to find a way to check on it that morning. She was hoping it hadn't been too frightened by the storm.

She slipped on clean shorts and a T-shirt, stepped over Gino and Pik and crept out of the bedroom. On the landing, where a cool breeze drifted from the open back door, she realised how stuffy and hot her bedroom had become and how, after only two nights, it already smelled like boys.

Jelly's mum was dressed and drinking coffee at the kitchen table. She looked up from the newspaper as Jelly came down the stairs. 'How are you feeling, love?'

'Better.'

'That's good.' She held out an arm and Jelly folded herself into her mother's side. She didn't bother reading the paper over her shoulder; there was never any good news. And even the comics weren't funny.

'I'm going to see Nonna.' Her mum stroked Jelly's cheek with the back of her hand. 'Do you want to come with me?'

Jelly couldn't think of anything she'd like more than to see Nonna with her own eyes, to spend the morning with her mum. But she was worried about the angel. Should she stay or should she go?

Part of her wanted to forget the angel was there, to pretend they had never found it; the responsibility had almost become more than she could bear. But she knew she couldn't leave it alone in the shed, and she didn't want Gino to look after it. She didn't want to give him any more reason to think it was his. Her mind whirred.

Perhaps they should take it back to the creek? Jelly didn't know how long it would be before she could get Stef over to see it. And maybe it wasn't such a good idea to show other people anyway? The longer they kept it the more chance that someone else would find it. Those Northbridge High boys. Or adults! Adults would take it away and want to do experiments on it or put it in a museum or something. She *couldn't* let that happen.

Zia's voice at the top of the stairs startled her out of her thoughts. She was calling for Jelly's mum in a low, urgent voice. Her mother shot up from the table and Jelly followed.

'It's Sophia,' Zia said, pulling at her hands. 'Come and see.'

They crept into the study where Sophia was sleeping and peered into her cot. Sophia's eyes were shut but her mouth was open and she was breathing quickly. Even in the half-light Jelly could see what Zia was worried about. Mum gasped. All over Sophia's skin, an angry rash had broken out. In places, it had blistered, and in the folds it was red and raw. Her dark hair was matted against her temples and sweat dribbled into the creases of her neck.

Jelly's mum put a hand on Sophia's forehead. 'She's burning up,' she said, her voice straining to remain calm. 'I think we should take her to the Children's. Jel, you'll have to stay here to help Dad with the boys.'

'But,' Jelly said, 'what about Nonna?'

Her mum frowned and Jelly flopped down onto the landing, filled with disappointment. She hadn't expected the decision to be made for her this way.

Within minutes they were gone. Jelly's dad helped them to the car then clumped back up the stairs in his boxer shorts. He sighed and roughed up Jelly's hair on the way back to bed. 'Strange days,' he said. 'Strange days.'

Gino appeared in the doorway of the bedroom. 'Where did Mum go?' he yawned.

'Sophia's sick,' Jelly said. 'They've taken her to hospital.'

'What's wrong with her? What happened?' The words tumbled out barely in the right order.

'How should I know?' She marched downstairs. 'I'm going to take the angel some food before the others get up. You can come or not.'

'Wait.' Gino ducked back into her room to get his shoes.

'Don't wake Pik,' Jelly warned.

The rain had turned the creek bank to mud and they skidded and slipped down to the bike path. The plastic bag Jelly had filled with grapes and apricots bumped against her thigh. The creek was high and the water roared furiously, dragging everything in its way. The family of ducks that lived near the tunnel were paddling hard not to be swept downstream, and the narrow beach where they had sat the day before had disappeared, swallowed by the storm.

Before they turned down the side of the school, she checked for Jack or Budgie, but there was no one about. As they drew close to the shed, Jelly heard a soft banging and scraping against the tin wall. They paused and Gino looked at Jelly.

'I think we should take it back to the creek,' she said.

'No way.'

'It doesn't belong to you, Gino.'

'Finders keepers. Remember?'

'That's stupid. I don't mean that. It doesn't belong to me either. What if it has a mother or something that's looking for it?'

'Angels don't have mothers.'

'How do you know? It's only a baby, Gino.'

'I can look after it.'

'How?'

'Same as you. I can look after it as good as you.'

'Look after it then!' Jelly thrust the plastic bag into Gino's hands. 'And if it dies it's *your* fault.'

She marched across the playground. At the fence, she turned to see Gino open the shed door and slide in. There was a wild flapping. She heard Gino shouting, then a crash. Jelly darted over. She opened the door just a crack, but the angel spotted her. It swept over and caught her hair in its hands, dragging her into the shed.

'Don't let it out!' Gino leapt up from where he was cowering on the floor and pulled the shed door behind her. The angel squatted on Jelly's shoulders, its mouth and fingers in her hair, toes digging into her shoulders. Jelly tried to shake it off, but the angel's wings rose and flapped wildly each time she moved. With every powerful swoop Jelly was nearly lifted off the ground. Then the angel squealed.

Jelly covered her ears and stumbled around the room. 'Let me go,' she begged the angel. 'Please let me go.' She tried to bat it from her head but it held on tightly.

Eventually the angel stopped its infernal shrieking. It clambered down her back and crawled in between her legs, wrapping its fingers around her ankles and glowering at Gino. Jelly lifted it to her chest. Both their hearts were pounding.

'What did you do to it?'

'I didn't do anything,' said Gino, still flattened against the door. There was a long pink scratch down his cheek and he was breathing fast.

Jelly carried the angel to the blanket and sat down. In the corner of the shed she noticed a small pile of shredded bandages. 'Well, at least its wing seems better.'

She couldn't help smiling as she handed a bunch of grapes to the angel. She had no idea why it had become so attached to her and not Gino. Right from when they had found it in the tunnel it had never let Gino or Pik get close. Perhaps it saw her as a mother figure? But that wouldn't explain why it shied away from the boys.

'We've got to be careful it doesn't get away,' Gino said, his eyes fixed on the angel fossicking around in the fruit bag. 'Now that it can fly again.'

'It's better, Gino. We should let it go. That's what we said.'

The angel spat grape skins and stalks into Jelly's lap and shoved a ripe apricot into its wet mouth. Jelly brushed the rubbish off her shorts.

'I told you, I'm keeping it. It only wants you 'cause it sees you. Yesterday it was fine with me after you left.'

'Even if that was true, what are you going to do with it? You can't keep it forever, Gino.'

'Why not?'

'Because it's…it's…it's not a pet.'

Gino flared up. 'Stop telling me what to do all the time. I'm sick of it. You're always bossing me around. It's not like you're even my friend—you're just my stupid cousin. You say my dad bosses me around but you're worse.'

Jelly stood up and shoved the angel into Gino's arms. 'Fine. Take it then!'

Jelly stormed out of the shed, pulling the door firmly behind her. She could hear the angel shrieking but she ran across the courtyard without stopping. Sliding under the fence she sheared off one of the new scabs on her knee and gasped. As she ran down the street, she let herself cry, but only for her knee.

Jelly turned away from the prying windows of an early morning tram as it clattered past. When she reached the bike path she slowed. Tears were running down her face and blood down her shin. She wiped her nose on the back of her hand. She didn't care what Gino said. She hated him. And his stupid family. Especially Zio Mario. She wished they'd go home and let her have her house back. She wished Nonna hadn't got sick and messed up Christmas and that they could just start all over again. She wished that Gino would let the angel go.

13

that boy again

Jelly climbed the back fence, her face still wet with tears. She swung herself up into the wide branches of the apricot tree and found the little hollow that was her perfect armchair. It was the only place she could bear to be. She rubbed at the smear of dried blood down her shin, and told herself she was better off without the angel. She didn't care what happened to it anymore. It was no longer her responsibility. If it died it would be Gino's fault. Not hers.

Someone at the creek caught her eye. It was that boy, walking along by the rushing water. Jelly watched him trail a long stick in the mud, swirling lines and jabbing holes. He stopped to lift up rubbish with his stick, found an old frisbee caught in the reeds, inspected it, and tucked it under his arm. Jelly liked watching him from up there. He walked slow and smooth, like someone with all the time in the world. Like someone who might have a tune in their head or a thought in their mind. Not like most people who followed the creek—joggers and cyclists and people with somewhere to go, rushing along, like the creek was only a path to follow, not a world to discover.

The boy suddenly looked up, shading his eyes with his hand. He was staring straight at her and for a moment she panicked that he might see her watching him, but his arm fell and he kept walking. There was something about looking at that boy that turned Jelly's stomach inside out. Where only moments before it was shrivelled like a dark black prune, it now fluttered with butterflies.

The good feeling disappeared when she saw Maureen at the back door. What was she doing here again? Didn't she have her own home? Little black thoughts came up easily and Jelly didn't try to stop them. They shot out of her like bullets.

'Jelly,' Maureen called. 'Gino, Pik.'

Jelly swung down from the tree.

'Thank goodness,' Maureen said. 'You gave me a fright. Your mum asked me to come over and keep an eye on you kids while she's gone. Where are Gino and Pik?'

'Gino's, er, gone for a walk.' Jelly limped up the back steps. 'Gone to pick some more flowers for Nonna, I think.'

'With Pik? He didn't take Pik down to the creek, did he?'

'No, Maureen,' Jelly said rudely. 'Pik's still in bed.'

Maureen put a hand on her shoulder. 'Pik is *not* in bed, Jelly.'

Jelly heard the words but it took a minute to understand what they meant. The realisation flooded through her, turning her blood cold. Jelly knew instantly what had happened.

Pik had woken and decided to follow them.

He knew where they were heading.

Down to the creek.

Jelly knew that she would be blamed. The oldest. The girl. It was always the way. So she did the only thing she could think of to save herself. She lied.

'Oh, he must have gone with Gino. They left after

93

me. We were going to the playground. But then I, um, fell over so I came back to get a bandaid.' She pointed to her crusty knee. 'They're probably still waiting for me. I'll go and get them.'

Maureen was watching her carefully. Jelly couldn't quite meet her eye. She stared at a mole just above her raised eyebrows.

'Off you go then,' Maureen said slowly. 'But hurry. I don't want you kids to still be out when your dad wakes up.'

Instead of climbing over the back fence, Jelly went out the side gate as if she was going to the playground. She rounded the side of Maureen's house and ran through her garden to cut through to the bike path. Her feet pounded the earth and her heart raced. She imagined Pik, swallowed up by the creek. She saw his face, deep in the cloudy water, his body tangled in the reeds, and then the face of the angel looking out at her in place of Pik's.

He won't have gone near the water, she tried to convince herself. It frightens him. He can't swim. He would've stuck to the path. He will be fine. He will be fine.

But the banks are so slippery, came a dark voice from inside her, *the creek so high*.

She skidded down the bank, clutching at bushes and reeds to slow her slide. A flock of cockatoos screeched overhead. She reached the path and began calling his name.

An early morning jogger was heading towards her. She wanted to ask if he'd seen a little boy, but felt too ashamed. It was all her fault. She had drowned Pik. And she had no idea how she could live with herself. The jogger passed, and tears streamed down her face.

'Pik!' she called. 'Pik, where *are* you?' She ran, but her eyes were so blurred with tears she could hardly see where she was going. She stumbled on, praying, praying that the worst hadn't happened. 'Please, please make Pik okay. Please let me find him. I will never have another mean thought. I will take that angel back to the creek somehow, even if Gino never speaks to me again.'

She reached the tunnel where everything had begun. There was no sign of Pik. Jelly hung her head in her hands. I can't do this on my own. I wish, wish, wish that someone was here to help me. She had never felt so alone.

Then she heard faraway voices echoing through the tunnel. She listened. Was that Pik? Talking to someone? She'd never loved the sound of his voice so much. Her heart leapt. His voice came again. Louder this time. 'There she is,' she heard him say. She looked up to see two figures coming through the tunnel, silhouetted against the slanting light.

Pik and the boy with the black hair walked into the daylight. They were holding hands and the boy smiled at Jelly.

'Pik!' she shouted. 'Where were you?'

'He was wandering along the track,' said the boy. 'A little too close to the water. Said he was looking for—'

'—angels,' Pik finished, smiling at his new friend.

'Yeah.' The boy shrugged. 'Says they're in the creek. But I told him that even if he did see one he should never try to catch it because it's bad luck to catch an angel, hey, Pik? You just leave them alone.'

Pik nodded. 'I didn't tell him you and Gino got one.'

'Nup,' the boy said, grinning. 'He didn't tell me that.'

'But I did tell him I couldn't find you,' Pik said, sniffing theatrically. 'I told him that you and Gino went off without me. Again!'

Jelly dried her eyes on the back of her hand and even though the boy was there she pulled Pik into

96

her arms so tight he gasped. 'You're naughty,' she said, laughing. 'You are *so* naughty, Pikky, I should smack you.' And then she tickled him so hard he squealed. She looked up at the boy. 'Thank you *so* much. I owe you one. You have no idea how much trouble I was going to be in.'

'Two,' the boy said, his smile bright. He flicked his fringe out of his eyes. 'Actually, that's two you owe me now, I believe.'

Jelly felt her cheeks heat up and she looked down at the ground. Her feet were spattered with mud.

'Tell her that other stuff about the angels.' Pik pulled away from her clasp and took the boy's hand.

The boy smiled and poked Pik. 'Nah, they're just made-up stories. No such thing as angels, remember?'

'But you said—' Pik frowned.

The boy handed Pik his stick. 'Here, I said you could have this when I was finished with it. You'd better go now. It's dangerous to play near the creek. A kid drowned here a couple of years ago.' He ran his hand through his hair then turned back the way he came.

Jelly watched him walk away then grabbed Pik's hand. 'Come on,' she said. 'Now we have to find Gino.'

Gino was walking down St Peter's Road when Pik and Jelly got to the bridge. She waved for him to hurry and he ran to catch up with them.

'We were in the park, okay?' She pulled Pik into a run alongside her. 'And, Pik, no more stuff about angels.'

Gino didn't say anything. Jelly glanced at him as they ran along the track to the playground. There were long scratches on his arm. He turned and caught her staring at him and she offered him a smile. But he only glowered at her, then looked straight ahead.

Jelly couldn't understand what had got into him. They'd fought in the past but it had never been like this before. It was like the Gino she knew was no longer there.

small comforts

They got back just in time for Maureen to serve up a batch of pancakes. She was humming along to some old song and skipping around in Nonna's apron again. Jelly wished she'd take it off; she was getting pancake mix all over it. But then Jelly remembered her promise by the creek to think nice thoughts.

'Thanks for making us pancakes, Maureen.'

Maureen looked taken aback. 'Well, that's all right, honey. I hope you like them.' She handed Jelly two plates. 'Take one of these up to your dad.'

'I'll eat mine with him.' Jelly flooded the pancakes

with maple syrup, happy to have an excuse to leave. She wasn't quite ready to test out her good-thought resolution on Gino.

Jelly's dad was awake when she got to his room. 'Hey, beautiful. Hop up here with me.' He patted the space beside him.

Jelly climbed onto the bed and snuggled in next to him. She could smell her mum on the pillow. Jelly's dad put his arm around her. 'Mum just called. Sophia has measles, that's all. They're bringing her home. Just as well. I don't think we could handle any more bad luck in this family right now.'

Jelly shoved a forkful of pancake into her mouth. 'What about Nonna?' she said, her mouth full.

Her dad sighed. 'We don't know yet.'

'What do you mean?'

There was a pause.

'Nonna's getting old, love.'

A lump of pancake stuck in Jelly's throat. 'What's that supposed to mean?'

Her dad ran his big hand over her head. 'Well, her body's getting tired.'

'She's coming home, though? Right?'

'I hope so, honey. I hope so.'

Jelly forced the pancake down.

'Mum also wanted to know if you'd still like to visit Nonna. She'll pick you up after she's taken Sophia and Zia back to their place to rest.'

Jelly nodded and leaned over to hug him. They stayed like that for what felt like ages. Finally, her dad pulled away. His eyes were wet. He gave Jelly a crumpled smile. 'She'll be happy to see you, love,' he said. 'Who knows? It might just be what she needs.'

This turned Jelly's mind to her other worry. 'Dad?' she said. 'If someone you knew—your friend—was doing something you didn't think was right, what would you do?'

'Why, honey?'

'No reason. Just asking.'

'Is someone you know in trouble?'

'*No*, Dad.'

'Well, what do you mean by "not right"?'

'Say this friend caught a wild bird, a big one, like a pelican, and wanted to keep it as a pet. But you knew that bird—the pelican, or another kind of big bird *like* a pelican—wasn't happy being kept as a pet, but your friend wanted to keep it, what would you do?'

'You remember what happened to that sulphur-crested cockatoo, love, even after we'd fixed its wing and you'd dug up grubs for it and looked after it? And you remember how upset you were, even though it wasn't your fault?'

Jelly nodded, remembering the cold stiff body at the bottom of the shoebox, the matted white feathers—nothing like the bird that had once squawked and chattered and flown.

'You know how I feel about wild birds, love.'

'Yeah,' Jelly said, and she did. And knowing that she and her dad felt the same way was some comfort.

15

the hospital

'Don't be frightened by how Nonna looks, darling,' Jelly's mum said quietly. 'The painkillers make her a little drowsy, so she might not seem herself.'

Jelly's stomach flipped around as a nurse ushered them along a squeaky linoleum corridor. She peered into some of the open rooms and saw old people sleeping or gazing up at television screens that hung from the ceilings. Their skinny bodies made hills and valleys in a landscape of pale blue cotton blankets. Surely her nonna couldn't look like that? Her mum's grip tightened around her hand.

'Mrs Mancini?' said the nurse as she entered a dark, quiet room. The curtain was drawn around the bed. 'Your family is here to see you.'

Jelly took a deep breath and peered around the curtain.

Nonna was sitting up in bed, watching TV with the sound down. When she saw them she snorted. '*Finalmente*! At last, some good visitors.'

'You're looking a little better today!' Jelly's mum said.

'Shall I pull back the curtain for you, Mrs Mancini?' the nurse asked.

Nonna shrugged. 'Open, close. I no care. It no matter to me. My eyes so bad it all the same.'

Jelly's mum rolled her eyes at the nurse. The nurse smiled and left the room.

'Hi, Nonna,' Jelly said, holding out the pink carnations they had bought at the florist downstairs.

'Come here, bella. Kiss you nonna.' She frowned. 'I no need flowers to get better. I just need my beautiful grandchildren.' Jelly kissed her grandmother dutifully on both velvety cheeks but Nonna pulled her into a fierce hug.

'Jelly, I'm going to talk to the doctors. I'll be back soon,' said her mum.

'Why you call her *Jelly*?' Nonna grumbled. 'She already have good name.'

Jelly's mum raised an eyebrow at her.

'I'll be fine,' Jelly said and hopped up onto Nonna's bed.

Nonna frowned. 'Course she be fine. What you think? Here, bella. Look in Nonna's bag. I have chocolates.'

Jelly's mum left the room and Nonna shuffled over to make room for Jelly against the mountain of crisp white pillows.

'I have TV in bed. Good, eh?' Then she leaned in and frowned. 'But food! Food is *disgustoso*! You nonna no can eat this food. Look how skinny you nonna get.' She pinched a roll of fat from her wide, wide stomach, and laughed. Jelly smiled to hear her nonna back in full form.

They watched some bad daytime TV for a while, without bothering to put the sound up. Nonna caressed Jelly's small hand in her big rough one, her fingers as knobbled as old grapevines. Jelly used to hate it when Nonna wanted to hold her hand all the time, especially when she was little, but now she didn't mind so much.

A big white bird wheeled past the window,

floating effortlessly against the sun-bleached sky. Jelly's thoughts turned to the angel. If anyone was to believe in angels it would be her nonna.

'Nonna,' she said. 'Have you ever seen an angel?'

Nonna tightened her grasp around Jelly's hand. 'No, *mia bella*. When you nonno die I think I no want to live. Me and you nonno, we together for sixty-three years. You imagine? I don't know how I live after he gone. Every day I pray to be with him. But when I get the heart pain the other night all I can think is I no ready. I no ready for my angel to come.'

Nonna cupped Jelly's cheek in her palm and her eyes filled with tears. 'Because I still have you, *mia bella*. And my other three beautiful grandchildren. I want to see you grow up. Then I happy to be with you nonno. Now, I no ready. I want to stay.' She slid her hand down again to find Jelly's. 'You my angel.' She turned back towards the television.

They watched the screen in silence and an ache rushed through Jelly's heart.

Was the angel here for her nonna? Is that why it had come? Why else had it turned up on Christmas Eve, the very night that Nonna had fallen ill? If she had left the angel in the creek that night would her nonna now be…? She couldn't bear to think about it.

The bird swooped back again, arcing and looping in the sky, and other thoughts filled her head. She remembered finding a butterfly in the garden when she was a little girl. She had picked it up by its wings and proudly carried it inside to show her dad. He had hugged her and explained that now she had touched the butterfly's wings it would no longer be able to fly. Even the most gentle touch damaged them beyond repair. Sometimes, he said, it is better to leave nature alone.

Jelly had refused to believe him. She climbed up into the lemon tree and placed the butterfly on the highest branch where it swayed in the breeze, and she sat there holding her breath, bursting with hope. But the butterfly toppled down to the ground like a piece of blackened paper.

16

the bad thing returns

That afternoon, Jelly stayed in her room while Gino and Pik watched TV downstairs. Gino and Jelly were still not speaking to each other. But Jelly didn't want to be the one to break the silence. He can make it up to me, she thought. He's the one who's wrong this time.

She took out her sketchbook and pencils to make a card for Nonna. She drew an angel on the front of the card with two outstretched wings. She thought of their little angel and drew its sweet face and long curling hair. She wondered if it was missing its mother. Surely angels had families? Why wouldn't they? Even animals had families.

Suddenly, her room darkened and she heard a rumble of thunder. Out the window indigo clouds gathered like bruises. There was a sound like a stone dropping onto the tin roof. Then another and another. Hail? In the middle of summer? Her wooden blinds clattered in the wind and she stood up to close the window. Through the glass there was a flash of lightning and the whole sky lit up. That's when Jelly saw it. In the light. Hovering above the apricot tree. It was so bright she could barely make out its face, but it was there. A figure. Long and tall with blinding eyes and wild, winding hair. And wings. Huge wings that filled the width of her window and more. Much bigger than their angel. Staring right at her. Then it was gone.

There was another crack of lightning and, as she watched, her dear old apricot tree split clean in two. The right side crashed onto the side fence, flattening it. The left side fell on Nonna's vegetable patch. Jelly heard her dad bounding down the stairs, shouting, Maureen's shrill voice in the kitchen, Pik squealing. The hail fell harder; its roar was deafening. Jelly watched her dad run out into the back garden, his hands in his hair. The wind whipped around him. Then the lights went out. Jelly felt a stabbing pain in her head and then something wet dripping onto her hand. There was another flash of lightning and when she looked down, she saw blood falling from her nose. She moved back from the window, sat on the edge of her bed and pinched her nose. The hailstones turned to slicing rain. In the kitchen, her dad was shouting at Maureen to find candles, for Gino and Pik to stay calm.

Eventually, her nosebleed stopped and the pain in her head lessened. She got up from her bed to find her shoes. In the dark of the storm, she slipped downstairs and out the back door. Her dad was lighting candles and Maureen was comforting Pik, who was wailing. No one saw her leave. She ran out into the garden and was soaked within seconds. She stood in front of the apricot tree, her old friend, and tears pricked her eyes. The trunk was scorched black and great splinters, as tall as Jelly, pointed to the sky. She scrambled over the fallen branches and headed to the creek. The rain drove into her body like needles and the wind pulled at her like hands. I have to stop this, she thought. There is only one way to stop this and I know now what I must do.

Water rushed down the embankment, and her feet slid out from under her. She had never seen the creek so fierce. It roared up like a dragon, spiky with rain. As she ran along the bike path, the sky cracked open again with light. On St Peter's Road, people were scurrying for shelter. A car skidded on the tram tracks. When Jelly reached Ivy Street, the rain suddenly cleared. The clouds rolled away and it was day again. She slowed to a walk, her breath coming in gasps. Blood was pounding in her head. One by one, people opened their front doors to stare up at the sky.

Now that it was light again Jelly began to wonder how she could possibly get the angel down to the creek. In broad daylight. And on her own. As if her fears had been spoken aloud, she saw two figures on bikes in the distance, winding their way towards her. Budgie and Jack. When they spotted her, Jack picked up speed and Budgie followed him. Jelly thought about turning back, but then they were beside her.

Jack rode his bike a full circle around her then skidded to a stop. 'You,' he said. 'Still hanging around.'

Budgie showed his yellow teeth.

Jelly said nothing. She had nothing to say.

'Didn't we tie you up tightly enough last time?' Jack dropped his bike to the ground and stepped over its shiny frame. He shoved his hands into his pockets and his elbows stuck out like wings. 'You're a pain, aren't you? Hanging around like a bad smell. Why do you keep coming here, anyhow? What's in the school that you're so interested in?'

Jelly looked at the ground. Rain dripped from her clothes onto the wet footpath. It trickled down the backs of her knees. 'I—' she started.

That's when they heard the sound. Banging on tin. Coming from the shed.

Jack chuckled. 'Ah, that's what it is then? You keeping something in there? You wanna come and show us?'

'There's nothing,' she said. 'That's just the tool shed. There's nothing in there.'

But she shouldn't have spoken. At the sound of her voice, the banging became louder.

'Really?' Jack grinned. 'Maybe we should see for ourselves.'

He stuck his foot under the wire and lifted it. Budgie leaned his bike against a pole and shoved Jelly aside as he passed. Jack slid under and Budgie went to follow him. For a moment Jelly wasn't sure he would get through, but then, with a grunt, he was on the other side. Jelly stood frozen to the footpath. Jack and Budgie sauntered over to the tool shed. As they neared it the banging stopped. Jelly's instinct told her to run away. She could save herself. She need never know what happened to the angel. She need never come back this way again. But she knew she couldn't do it. It was her fault the angel was trapped. She couldn't leave it to Jack and Budgie.

She watched them pause at the shed door. Jack opened it and peered in. All was quiet. Budgie nudged him and the two boys stepped into the shed. Suddenly the door slammed shut and there was a wild scream. At first she thought it was the angel and her blood ran cold. She slid under the fence and ran towards them. They were hurting it! But then the scream came again and she knew it wasn't the angel. It was a boy's voice. There was a crashing sound and more banging. She ran to the shed door and pulled at it, but it wouldn't open.

'Let me in!' she shouted. 'Don't hurt it. Let me in.'

Suddenly the door swung open, catching her in the face, and she stumbled backwards. She looked up to see who was coming out. It was Gino! He had the picnic blanket in his arms and he shoved it at

Jelly. Then he slammed the door shut and bolted it. 'Quick,' he said. 'You take it.'

The blanket began to scrabble in her arms. A long white arm reached out, then the angel's head burst through the folds.

Jelly's mind was spinning. 'What's going on?'

'Hurry! Before they break the door down.' Gino leaned against the door, which was rocking on its hinges as Jack and Budgie thumped and shouted to be let out. 'Go! I can't hold these guys in for much longer. And I sure don't want to be here when they get out. Go! I'll head home to cover for you.'

Jelly raced to the fence. As she ran down Ivy Street it began to rain again. Lightly at first, then harder and harder. The cold rain seemed to soak through her skin and course through her veins. She saw a vision of Nonna in hospital, lying on her stiff white bed. A bright light flashed at her window. It was an angel. No, it couldn't be. Nonna wasn't ready. She wasn't ready to go. The angel couldn't be here for her. But then Jelly wondered if you really got a say in these things. Her feet carried her towards the creek. She didn't know where else to go, what else to do.

She reached the bike path and slowed so as not to slip, but as they neared the water the angel grew restless in her arms. It pushed out from the blanket and Jelly toppled over, trying to keep hold of it. She landed hard on her injured knees and roared out in pain. The angel scrambled over her, panicking, and scuttled towards the road.

'No,' Jelly shouted, and pulled herself up. 'Not that way!'

Jelly grabbed at its leg but the angel's skin was slippery with rain and it slid from her grasp. Quickly, she picked up the picnic blanket and tossed it over the angel. The weight of the wet blanket threw it to the ground. She pounced on it, rolled it tightly again and lifted it up. Her knees were bleeding and she limped towards the creek.

The tunnel waited, mouth wide. Jelly carried the angel inside where no one could see them. The rain was so heavy that there was little risk of anyone being on the bike path and she was hidden from the road by the bridge. A tram clacked overhead. Here, in the gloomy light, she let the blanket fall away from the angel's face. It looked up at her and she saw that its glassy eyes were calm. She knew that this was the right thing to do. The only thing to do. And she prayed that all the bad things would stop when the angel was returned. That whatever was looking for it, that thing in the light in her window, that thing that killed her tree, that got in her head, that made Nonna sick, would go away and leave them alone once the angel was safely back where it belonged.

Jelly waded into the water with the angel in her arms. The creek was much higher than it had been the night they found the angel. It pushed and pulled her deeper. When she reached the place where the rock was, now deep under the swirling water, she unwrapped the blanket. It was wrenched away from her and floated downstream.

'Go,' she whispered to the angel. 'Go!' The angel clung to her as it unfurled its enormous wings. They gleamed in the shadows. It beat them twice. Two slow beats and Jelly felt herself lifting upwards. Then her heart sank as it occurred to her that she was wrong. The bad thing was there. Right there in the tunnel, in the darkness, in the creek. The water reared up. A blinding light filled the tunnel and her head filled with pain. She felt her arms empty, her head grow light, then she sank into black.

At that moment Jelly knew for certain.

The angel had not come for her nonna.

The angel had come for her.

17

the dark, the light

Jelly woke. She opened her eyes. She was lying in the mud of the creek bank in the dark of the tunnel. She didn't know how or why but she had been saved. She was safe. The rain had stopped and the creek rushed past her feet, lapping at her shoes. But she was still there. Her body was hollow but her heart was full. In the distance she heard footsteps running towards her. She turned her head slowly and in the entrance she saw two figures silhouetted against the bright light of the day. Her dad rushed towards her, scooped her up into his arms. His face was wet. 'Oh, my baby,' he buried his head against her neck. 'Oh, my baby girl. I couldn't bear it if anything happened to you.'

He swung her up into his arms just like when she was a child and held her, her head against his neck. Jelly felt his chest heave. Then he turned back towards the entrance of the tunnel. 'Where is he? Where's that boy?'

But he was gone.

I owe you three times now, she thought.

18

the power of wishes

Jelly's dad changed her out of her wet clothes and tucked her into bed. Maureen brought her a hot chocolate and Gino and Pik hung about in the doorway.

'She needs to rest now,' her dad said. 'You boys can see her later.' He sat on Jelly's bed.

'Does Mum know?' she whispered.

Dad nodded. 'I called her.'

'I—I slipped...' It was the only thing she could think of to say.

'It's okay,' he said. 'For now all I care about is that you're safe.' He stroked her forehead. She closed her eyes. When she opened them again his eyes were shiny with tears.

Dad stood up to close her blinds and she lay on her bed in the dark. He left the room and she heard him on the upstairs phone to Mum. She thought she heard him crying. She had only heard her dad cry like that once before. Eight years ago. When his father had died. She closed her eyes and prayed that Nonna was all right.

She wished everyone would just come home.

Jelly drifted in and out of sleep. Sometimes she woke and her dad was sitting next to her in the dark. She heard her mum come home. She came quietly into Jelly's room and kissed her forehead. She heard Gino and Pik get into their beds on the floor.

She was there but also not.

Soon the house was quiet.

She fell into a dream-filled sleep.

The baby angel was sitting at the end of her bed. It crouched there, knees tucked under its chin, peeling grapes and popping them into its mouth. When it realised Jelly was watching, the angel smiled and passed Jelly a grape. Jelly looked down at the smooth grape in her open palm. As she watched, the grape began to grow. Its translucent sides split open and hundreds of tiny silver angels, each one no bigger than a firefly, spun into the air. As they reached the open window they drifted up into the night sky where they spread out across the darkness, glittering like stars.

The next morning, Jelly woke with the birds. They were singing loud and bright around her window and the sun crept through the slats of her blinds. She lay awake and listened to Pik and Gino sleeping.

'Gino,' she hissed. She leaned over and shook him gently till he stirred.

'Hmm?'

'Shh, don't wake Pik.'

'What is it? Are you okay?'

'Yeah, I'm fine.' Jelly smiled. 'What happened in the shed yesterday? With Budgie and Jack?'

Gino sat up, rubbing his eyes. He grinned, his whole face lighting up. 'The angel scared those guys to bits. You should've seen it. It was more like a devil than an angel. I had been trying to get it to come to me when they came in, and when it saw them it just freaked. It was flapping everywhere like crazy. Lucky I got it in the blanket before they realised what it was.'

'What were you doing in there, anyway? Why were you trying to catch it?'

Gino was silent a moment. Then he took a deep breath and looked down. 'I saw it too. That thing in the lightning. It was the same as the thing in the water, wasn't it? Looking for our angel. I'd already begun to think that all the bad things happening weren't just a coincidence. Guess I just didn't want to believe it at first.' His voice became soft. 'I guess I was hoping I could get it to do stuff for me like it was doing for you.'

Jelly frowned. 'What are you talking about?'

'You really didn't notice? Your wishes. Every time you wished for something you got it. Sophia getting sick. I bet you wished for something that made the branch fall on Dad's car.'

'Why would I want Sophia to get sick? Are you crazy?'

'Well, you didn't wish for it exactly. But the angel made them happen that way. You wanted to keep the pram, remember? So you said you wished Sophia wasn't around. You see?'

Jelly felt a wave of nausea rush through her. It was me? she thought. It was me making all those bad things happen? Then she remembered. Nonna. She had made Nonna sick. She knew that now. When she wished for Gino to stay. All the bad thoughts she'd been having. She couldn't believe it. What other careless wishes had she made?

She looked up at Gino and he seemed to understand what was going through Jelly's mind. 'It's not your fault. You didn't know. I guessed what was happening but I didn't tell you because I wanted to get it to do stuff for me. But it wouldn't. Not even one wish. It wouldn't even let me touch it.'

Jelly remembered an old Italian saying her nonno had told her when she was young. She didn't know why she hadn't remembered it before. To see an angel meant someone would die. The angel *had* come for her. It really was her angel. That was why it wouldn't let Gino or Pik get close to it. But why hadn't it taken her away with it? Why had she been saved? Her mind spun with questions she knew she would never find an answer to.

'It was a good thing we took it back to the creek. Imagine if you'd got hold of it, Gino.' She smiled. 'What would you have wished for? Super powers?

All the money in the world? No, I know. You would have wished for that motorbike that your dad won't let you have. That Ducati Monster, or whatever it's called, right?' She giggled.

Gino looked away.

'Sorry,' Jelly said. 'Tell me. I think I know anyway. You would've wished your dad wasn't so angry all the time, right?'

Gino shrugged and Jelly squeezed his hand.

'Or that I'd stop bossing you around?' she said quietly.

'Nah,' said Gino, punching her in the shoulder. 'That's your job. Chief Pain in the Arse!'

'You can talk.' She punched Gino back and they both burst out laughing.

Pik sat up. 'What's so funny?'

'You, Pik,' Gino said. 'Your head's on backwards. Look!'

Pik frowned and patted his head and Gino and Jelly snorted with laughter.

There was a knock on the bedroom door. 'You kids awake?' Jelly's dad called out.

'Yeah.'

'Come downstairs then. We've got a surprise for you.'

The door swung open and light streamed into the bedroom. Both Jelly and Gino's parents were in the doorway, grinning. Zia Pia had baby Sophia on her hip. Sophia's cheeks were covered in crusty sores but she was back to her cranky self again, frowning and pulling at Zia's hair.

Pik clambered over Jelly's bed.

'Come and see the tree,' Jelly's mum said.

'Presents!' Pik shouted.

'Yep,' said Dad. 'Santa's come.'

Zia Pia passed Sophia to Zio Mario so she could cuddle Pik.

'And,' said Dad, 'we've got an extra special Christmas surprise. Come downstairs and see.'

They ran downstairs and there, sitting on the couch with a rug over her knee, was Nonna. She smiled and opened her arms wide to fold them all in.

'Careful with you nonna,' she scolded, as Pik clambered into her lap. 'You kids send me back to hospital again if you no careful.'

Jelly let Nonna pinch her cheeks mercilessly and cover her with kisses. Thank you, she said to the angel under her breath. Of all her accidental wishes, this was one she was truly grateful for.

'Well,' said Dad, clapping his hands together.

'Who's going to hand out the presents?'

'Me,' said Pik.

They sat down under the tree, three days late, and ripped open their presents. Jelly had a new art set from Mum, a book about birds from Dad, and Zia Pia had bought her a pink lacy bra, which she was quick to hide in the pocket of her pyjamas before Gino spotted it. Zia winked at her and she felt her cheeks burn. Then Gino handed Jelly his badly wrapped package and Jelly did her best to pretend she had never seen it before. But she had no trouble showing her delight when she pulled out the silver heart necklace. She threw her arms around Gino's neck and he grinned and shook her off.

'You're the best,' she said.

'I know,' said Gino.

Jelly tossed a ball of scrunched-up paper at him. She handed him his present and he unwrapped the disposable camera. 'Wish we'd had this a couple of days ago,' he said.

They shared a secret smile.

Pik got a blow-up swimming ring and Gino got a toolkit from his dad, with a real hammer and nails. 'Thought you might like to start helping me out in the shed,' Zio Mario said, awkwardly. Gino nodded.

All the kids got lumpy hand-knitted jumpers from Nonna, like they did every year, but this year they put them on to make her happy. Jelly's was too big and Gino's was too small. But Jelly figured it wasn't Nonna's fault, it wasn't just her who saw them that way.

It may have been three days late but it was the best Christmas ever. Everyone was so happy just to be together and especially to have Nonna home. Finally, they got to finish Nonna's special cake that had been waiting for them in the fridge since Christmas Eve. When all the dishes had been washed and put away and Nonna was dozing in front of the news in her special chair, like she usually did, it was time, finally, for everybody to go home.

'Bet you'll miss me,' Gino said to Jelly at the front door.

'Yeah, I was almost beginning to enjoy that smell in my room,' Jelly replied. 'Maybe you could just leave me a pair of your old socks till next time?'

Gino grinned and punched her arm as he pushed his way past.

'See you, Pik,' Jelly said, stooping to hug her little cousin.

He stood on his toes and his breath was warm in

her ear. 'Don't catch another angel without me, will you?'

'Of course not,' Jelly whispered back. 'Though next time we'll look for dragons, okay?'

Pik's eyes widened.

Jelly giggled. 'No such thing as dragons, Pik.'

But he eyed her suspiciously. 'That's what you said about angels.'

Jelly shrugged. 'You're right, Pik. You never know.'

Jelly watched Zio Mario back out of the driveway in his dented car, and smiled as he turned out of Rosemary Street. Perhaps the new house was going to be more interesting than she had first thought. She went upstairs to air out her bedroom.

19

a white feather

That evening, Jelly stood at her bedroom window gazing out at the blackened apricot tree, crumpled over the garden. The light was softening, the cicadas had started up and birds hopped around the apricots strewn across the lawn. She missed the tree. But Dad said they only lived so many years and it was due to come down soon anyway. Tomorrow they would go to the nursery to pick out a sapling to plant in its place. Nonna wanted a fig tree, Mum wanted a pear, but Dad and Jelly had already decided they would put in a flowering eucalypt to attract the cockatoos.

They weren't great for climbing, but Jelly figured by the time it was big enough to hold her she'd be too old to climb trees anyway. Maybe.

As she turned from the window to get into her pyjamas, Jelly spied someone down at her back fence. She pressed her face against the glass and peered out into the gathering gloom. It was that boy. Waving. Beckoning her to go down. Her heart skipped a beat. She went downstairs and out the back door. Her mum and dad were sitting out on the patio, sharing a bottle of wine and looking out over the destroyed garden.

'Where are you off to then, young lady?' her dad began, but her mum had seen the boy at the fence and she gave him a gentle nudge. 'Oh,' he said. 'Well, okay. But don't be out when it's dark.'

Jelly ran across the garden then slowed to catch her breath before she reached the fence.

'Hey,' she said, trying to hold back a grin.

'Hey,' the boy said back. 'How are you?'

'Fine. Yeah, fine.'

He glanced over her shoulder to where her parents were watching them. She turned and her mum and dad quickly bowed their heads together to pretend they were still talking.

'Can you come down to the creek for a bit?' he said. 'I've got something for you.'

'Sure,' she said and climbed onto the fence. She called out to her parents, 'Don't worry, I'll be back before it gets dark.'

Her dad stood up. 'You're not going down to the creek?'

But her mum put her hand on his arm and he sat down again, his brow furrowing. Jelly gave them a brisk wave and dropped down onto the other side.

'So,' she said, 'what is it?' She hadn't noticed before but his eyes were as dark as the night.

'Over here,' the boy said, and they slid down the creek bank. At the edge of the water he lifted up a large piece of bark and underneath was something long and flat, wrapped in brown paper. He pulled it out gently and handed it to her. 'Merry Christmas,' he said, smiling.

Jelly sat down to unwrap the paper. There, lying in her lap, was a white feather, the length of her arm. In the evening light it gleamed silver.

She gasped. 'You *saw* it?'

He looked into her eyes and nodded, then blushed. 'I was sheltering in the tunnel from the rain.'

'You saw the angel?'

'I thought that's what it was. I saw you carry it into the water. But then it got so bright I could hardly see a thing. I had to close my eyes because of the light.' He smiled. 'I knew you were up to something but I had no idea *that's* what you were hiding in the shed.'

Jelly poked her toe into the crumbly dirt. 'So it was you who pulled me out of the water?'

The boy shook his head. 'It all happened so quickly. When I opened my eyes you were already by the side of the creek. I went to get your dad, that's all. It wasn't me who pulled you out.'

Jelly looked out over the creek. It had already shrunk over the course of the day. The water swirled around the rocks the colour of chocolate milk and lapped gently at the bank. So different from the night before. She shivered.

'You think it was the angel who saved me?'

'There was no other way you could have got out of the water. But I don't think it was your little one, judging by the length of this feather. I reckon it was something bigger. Much bigger.'

Its mother, Jelly thought, and she realised she had known this all along. She must have been desperate to get her baby back. And all those signs. All those times she was trying to speak to me. How angry she must have been. But in the end, even though we took her baby, she saved me.

'But—but why? I thought if you saw an angel, that meant…' The thought had become too frightening for words. 'I thought it had come to take me away,' she said, looking down at her hands.

'I know. But I think this was a different kind of angel. They're not the same as the ones you're talking about.'

'What do you mean?'

The boy ran his hand through his hair. 'It's not the first time I've seen one like that. I saw one once before. Two years back. The day Johnno drowned.'

'You knew him? The kid that drowned in the creek?'

The boy nodded. 'He was my best friend. We were playing in the drains together when the rain came. I should have drowned too. I never knew who saved me. At least not for sure. My grandad told me it must've been a creek angel.' He smiled, and touched the feather gently with his long brown finger. 'Guess I never believed him till now.'

'A creek angel?'

'That's what he calls them, anyway. Reckons there are all kinds of angels, not just the ones, you know, that come and get you when you die. He reckons you can find them everywhere. If you're looking hard enough.'

Jelly sat and watched the Merri Creek rushing towards the sea. She tried to imagine all the other things that lived in there, other than the ducks and bugs and frogs. Some things even she found hard to imagine. Then she tried to picture a world full of angels and somehow it didn't feel as crazy as it sounded. She looked at the boy and he smiled at her. Like he knew exactly what she was thinking.

And she realised it wasn't only her bad wishes that had come true.

'Jelly, time to come inside now.' Dad's voice came from behind the fence.

Jelly felt her cheeks heat up. 'Better go,' she said. 'I don't want to push my luck after what happened yesterday. I still have some major explaining to do.' Jelly stood up and brushed off her shorts.

'*Jelly*? That's your name?'

She laughed. 'Well, kind of. It's short for Angelica. It's my grandmother's name.'

'Angelica's a nice name. Sounds like angel.' The boy smiled and passed her the feather. She tucked it down her T-shirt. She would put it in the top drawer of her dresser, next to the silver locket.

'I suppose so. It just sounds like a grandmother's name to me. Actually I've been thinking of calling myself Ange next year. When I start high school. Jelly's kind of a kid's name.'

'Ange is nice. Suits you.'

Jelly looked down at her feet to hide her smile.

'You starting high school next year?' he asked as they climbed up the steep embankment.

'Yeah.'

'Where?'

'Northbridge High.'

'Really? That's where I go.'

'Really?'

'Yeah. It's not bad. As far as schools go. You'll like it. I can introduce you to my friends, if you like. They're all skateboarders, though. Hope you like skateboarding.'

'Yeah, I do. Like skateboarding, I mean.' She paused. 'Your friends. You mean Jack and Budgie?'

'Nah, Budgie's my cousin, that's all. Our families just hang out over Christmas. He's okay. Jack's a bit of a loser, though. It's not like we hang out at school or anything. You'll see. That's the good thing about a big school. Plenty of people to choose from.'

'Jelly!' Dad called again.

'You'd better go.'

'Hey, what about you?' she said, turning to face him. In the darkening light his skin had turned gold. 'You haven't told me your name yet.'

'My real name—or my nickname?' He smiled.

'Both. Either. I don't mind.'

'Well, Giacometti's my real name.'

'*Giacometti?*'

He grinned. 'Named after my grandfather.'

She laughed. 'So your nickname's Jack, right?'

'Nah, that's what we call Grandad. My friends call me Spook.'

'Spook. Suits you.' She giggled. 'Guess I'll see you round then, Spook?' She hauled herself up onto the fence.

'Guess you will,' he said, grinning.

Jelly's dad moved away quickly as she came over the fence.

'Dad!' she frowned. 'Have you been listening?'

'No,' said her dad, pretending to be insulted. 'I was just…on my way to see your nonna. Her light's still on. Do you want to come with me?'

'Sure,' Jelly said, leaning into him. 'I'd like that.'

'I'm sure Nonna would like that, too.' Her dad

dropped his arm over her shoulder and winked. 'So, how'd it go?'

'*Dad*.'

'Just asking.'

Jelly's dad smiled and pulled her into a hug. Then she slipped her hand into his. They wandered through the gathering darkness towards the small square of light.

acknowledgments

For such a small book there are an extraordinary number of people I need to thank. First of all, Penny Hueston for her patience and faith, and Ali Arnold for her incisive editing, done always with the gentlest touch. Chong Wengho for his stunning cover, Susan Miller for the page design, and the whole Text gang for being amazing in everything they do.

Sallie Muirden was one of my first readers, followed by the fabulous Antoni Jach and my wonderful MC2 writers group: Rachel Power, George Dunford, Kathy Kizlos, Tasha Haines, Jacinta Halloran, Meredith Jelbert, Susan Paterson, Anna Dusk, Jane Sullivan, and Kim Kane, in particular, for her excellent feedback.

The seeds of this novel were planted way back, during a residency at Varuna, for which I am extremely grateful. To my fellow Varunians: Steve Axelson, Kate Cole-Adams, Sandy Bigna and Fiona Wood, and of course the archangel of Varuna, Peter Bishop.

Cassandra Austin and Martine Murray are my dearest friends and kindest readers. Andy Griffiths and Markus Zusak keep my chin up when clouds of doubt rumble overhead.

Thanks also to Jan Robertson and the PLC readers, including: Greta, Candice, Alexandra, Naomi, Kirsten, Caitlin and Thy, for their brilliant feedback and beautiful drawings. Special thanks also to Carmel Hyland and the wonderful Merri Creek Primary students who gave up their lunchtimes to hear me read this story aloud.

Last of all, but most importantly: my sisters and mother for reading this by the pool in Penang, my darling Max for reading this in the hammock in our backyard and my beloved Raffaele for holding my hand every step of the way.